EVERY SOUL

By LK Collins

DEDICATION

For Eric – I miss you every day.

"Learn from yesterday,

Live for today,

Hope for tomorrow."

—*Albert Einstein*

PROLOGUE

-Bain-

I hate that it has to be this way, and I'm sorry to have to tell you like this, but I've battled with this decision for so long. I can't take it anymore, Bain. I just can't. Please know how much I love you. You're my brother, and no matter what, you always will be. Just because I'm not there, doesn't mean I'm not with you. I know this is hard to accept, but for me, please try. The pain of this world is too great, compared to what's waiting for me on the other side. I know this will relieve my struggle – it has to. Love, Kinsey.

Reading her suicide note again kills me. I still can't come to terms with what she did. After Kinsey took her life, every day that passes I hope I'll find some answers. Except I haven't and I fear…I never will.

Staring at my unfamiliar reflection in the mirror, I'm pissed at the man I've become. I barely recognize my own face or remember who I used to be. I ease my pain the only way I know how and pop a few pills. As the white chalk dissolves on my tongue, I relish the flavor and know soon I will boost sky high.

"Bain," my mother calls from downstairs. *Jesus mother-fucking Christ, what does she want now?* If you think *I've* gotten bad since losing Kinsey, take a look at her – she's farther off the deep end than I'll ever be. Pulling my towel from my waist, I find a clean pair of boxers and jeans, this only thanks to our housekeeper.

Just as I exit my room, my mother is struggling up the stairs. I run to help her, but she gives up and falls face first onto the thick, cream carpet. I've seen her do this so many times that it's no surprise, so I settle next to her, resting my hand on top of her messy, blonde hair. She used to be so well kept, and now doesn't resemble her former self at all. "How much have you had to drink today?" I ask her.

She doesn't answer me, instead shaking her head so I know she heard me. "The investigator called," she slurs.

My stomach drops and a wave of nausea takes over. I know exactly what this means. Since my sister died, all we have is her assumed suicide note, which she texted to me. Besides that, the case has run dry – her body has not been found and there are no leads. We hold out hope that she's still alive somewhere.

Barely able to choke out the words, I ask, "What did he say?" There's a crackle to my voice, the pain cutting me deep within. This is not something I want to know, but I have to.

She begins to sob and rolls to her side, resting her hand on her forehead. Her cries turn to wails, and I know what she can't say. The reality of knowing she is really gone is a tremendous blow. Deep down, I'd hoped against hope that she was still alive. But all along I knew it wasn't true. We are fraternal twins, and when you lose that connection to your other half, you feel it.

She tries to speak, "They...He said..." She trails off crying, and in that moment, I don't know what else to do except to hold her. Lifting her fragile body onto my lap, I cradle her against the bare skin of my chest and just let her be. Then somehow she finds the courage to speak the words, the words I've feared for months. "She's dead, Bain. They found her."

Even though in my heart I've known it, the words kill me, tearing apart my insides. Tears break the rims of my eyes. My tortured mind drifts, picturing her dead body, bloody and mangled. I immediately wonder how she killed herself. I'm spinning from the combination of my thoughts and the pills. Then my mom clambers off of me and darts into the bathroom. She gets sick and I...I slink away.

I know I should be there for her, but I need answers. I have to know what happened. I grab a faded, gray t-shirt and my car keys, and then bolt. Starting the engine of my car, I blast the heat. It's another cold spring day in New Jersey, and of course I forgot my coat. Driving over the speed limit, I head to my familiar destination – the police station.

I reach for my phone out of habit, but it's not in the

cup holder. I pat both of my pockets and it's not there either. *Sonofabitch.* I guess I'll have to show up unannounced and hope that the ever incompetent detective will see me.

The last time that I was at the station, Detective Eldridge and I got into it. I accused him of letting the case go, of not taking things seriously. Needless to say, he didn't like hearing that. However, I'm not one to hold back, especially when it comes to my family. I felt like he could be doing more and I let him know that.

The drive only takes me fifteen minutes. I put my car in park and notice a few snowflakes starting to fall. This was Kinsey's favorite time of year. She always loved when the flowers would get covered in soft flakes. Now every time it begins to snow, I can't help but think of her. From the smells of an impending snow, to the chill it leaves on your skin, it all reminds me of her.

Looking in my backseat, I'm thankful to see a hoodie. Now I won't get the "tattoo looks" walking in. Besides, this prick already hates me. I grab it and put it on as I head inside the long, gray building. Two officers exit and one holds the door for me. The instant I walk inside, my senses are invaded by something so familiar. It all takes me back to that day…

"What do you mean I can't file a missing person's case? My sister never came home and I can't get ahold of her. What more proof do you need?"

"I'm sorry, Mr…?"

"*Adams,*" I snap back.

"*Mr. Adams, without any proof of foul play, we have to wait at least twenty-four hours.*"

"*That's fucking bullshit,*" I yell.

The woman sulks in her chair and a tall, salt-and-pepper haired man stands from a desk in the back. He walks over to us and asks, "*Is there a problem here, son?*"

"*Yeah, my sister is missing and for some God unknown reason this woman won't let me file a missing person's report until it's been twenty-four hours.*"

"*How old is she?*"

"*Twenty-two.*"

"*Do you have any proof of foul play?*" *I shake my head knowing exactly where this is going.*

"*I'm sorry, but unless she is a minor, state law requires us to wait at least twenty-four hours. Here is my card; if she doesn't come home, please call me directly.*"

I snatch the card out of his hand and look him straight in the eyes. My breathing is harsh and his disregard doesn't make anything better. I have a short fuse, always have. The last thing I need to do is assault a police officer...

"Mr. Adams, I was expecting you. How's your mom?" he asks.

"She's not well, and your phone call didn't make things any better."

"I apologize about that. Come with me, I assume you have some questions."

I nod my head following Detective Eldridge to one of

the back interrogation rooms. He opens the wooden door for me, and I take a seat in one of the dark blue, cloth chairs.

He sits across from me and crosses his hands on the table waiting for me to speak. Staring down at the rough carpet I ask, "Is she here?"

He shakes his head and responds softly, "No."

Bringing my pain-filled eyes up to meet his, the tears well and I don't know why. It's not like I wanted to see her, but part of me found comfort in thinking we were in the same building.

"What happened?"

"Are you sure you want to get into this without your parents here?"

"Yes," I snap and slam my fist on the table. "My mom told you from the beginning that she wants *you* to tell *me* everything."

"Calm down, Mr. Adams, I just wanted to ask. Your sister was found off of Old John's Road in a vacant home. From what we can tell, she broke in and parked her car in the garage."

I inhale sharply at his words.

"There was a hose that went into the driver's window of her car and the vehicle ran 'til it was out of gas."

My mind slips thinking of Kinsey breaking into a house. Parking inside some random garage. Killing herself by feeding a hose through her car window.

"When are you going to do an autopsy?"

"We're not."

"Goddammit, you have to. She didn't do this to herself. Kinsey wouldn't have."

"Mr. Adams, I understand how hard this must be for you. But this is a clear case of suicide. There is no reason to do an autopsy; please let your sister rest in peace. She *made* this decision."

"Fuck you, she didn't make this decision."

CHAPTER 1

-Bain-

In life, it is said that everything happens for a reason. If that's true, how can you explain death? What's the reason? Especially when it happens to someone so young, so beautiful, and so innocent? I struggle with these thoughts every day.

It's been six months since Kinsey's body was found and I mask the pain the only way I know how – by obsessing and losing myself over her death. Glancing at the clock, I've been staring at my laptop for over five hours. Fuck, where did the time go? I can't do this anymore. I need to get away.

I dial Jamison on my way out. He doesn't answer, so I shoot him a text.

What up, man, I'm all out and need a downer.

I wait a few minutes and watch the time on the clock tick by. It moves slowly, yet looking back, it's passed in the blink of an eye.

Since I know my dad will be home soon, I just start to drive out of my New Jersey neighborhood, weaving through the streets that are thickly lined with trees. Tiny snowflakes swirl around as I stare out my windshield – my destination as of now…unknown.

That is 'til a text message chimes in. I glance down, as I pull up to a stop sign.

I got something you'll like. They'll run ya fifteen bucks a pill, but worth it.

I'll take 'em all.

Meet me at my place in twenty.

Be there soon, I respond back and head to the bank before Jamison's. I went to high school with him, but we weren't friends back then, because I always swore that shit off, and he's been dealing for years. Recently I'd injured my knee, and until Kinsey passed, I'd been ultra-responsible with the pills. But since she went missing they've become my lifeline and my sanity. Then when I was pushing the limits on my refills, my doctor wanted to check my knee. All it took was one look and he said I didn't need them anymore. Everything's spiraled from there. So I found Jamison, and sure enough, he's still in the game.

It's not long 'til I arrive at his house. I put a thousand dollars in my wallet and leave the rest in my center console. My feet hit the pavement with a purpose and I observe my surroundings as I cross the street. He lives in a nice neighborhood with older, well-kept homes.

I ring the doorbell and immediately hear his two dogs bark. They are Rottweilers, which look scary as fuck, but are really two huge babies. He answers and commands them both to their beds. Right away they listen and then I walk in.

"What up, bro?" he asks, giving me a low fist bump.

"Not much. Thanks for getting back to me so fast."

"You're my best client." He begins to walk to his living room and gestures that I follow. Jamison is way shorter than I am, probably by a foot. Then again I am over six feet. He's dressed the same way he was in high school – big, baggy pants and some stupid ass t-shirt.

"You ever heard of Quaaludes?" he asks as we sit in front of the table filled with pill bottles.

"Nah, what are they?"

"Basically a tranquilizer. They're super old school, you can't even get them through a doctor in the US anymore."

I can't help but laugh out loud. I know I wanted a downer, but this seems a bit extreme. "I wanna be able to function, not knock my dick in the dirt."

"I know. I heard what you said and I got some Xanax coming for that. But I was thinking if the Hydro isn't giving you enough of a high, you could try the 'ludes. All you have to do is stay awake through the first fifteen minutes or so and after that, the effects kick in. It's an intense, euphoric high."

"I don't know, man. Maybe I'll just stick with what I

have."

"Why don't you try one now? While I'm waiting on the bars to get here."

The Hydro I knocked back earlier has worn off and I know I need something. "How long 'til they're here?"

Jamison checks his phone. "Not long, he just texted me that he should be here any minute."

"I'll wait then," I respond.

"So, no 'ludes?"

"Have you tried them?"

"Fuck yeah, I have. They are my drug of choice."

I rest my head back contemplating his words. I promised myself from the beginning that when I started taking pills, I would always stay functional and in control. I want to be able to be around my parents and shit like that. This could jeopardize –everything.

"I'm good, bro. Do you have any bars at all while we wait?"

"Nah, man, but he'll be here any minute, I promise."

CHAPTER 2

-Arion-

"Whatcha waiting for?" Brady calls from behind me. He's stark naked and gripping his cock.

I exhale and lock the door, ripping my shirt over my head. Leaving my reality and getting lost in this moment with him. Beginning to walk towards him, he's got the biggest grin on his face. "Take your pants off," he orders. I listen, tugging my jeans down, leaving only my underwear and bra on. I know him well and he loves to take these off himself.

Although we are a little drunk, we still have fun. That's one of the reasons why I keep Brady around. There are no strings – just sex. And that's all I've looked for lately. There is something about the accomplishment of luring in a guy and having my way with him. Then being able to make the decision whether there is a next time or not. Which most of the time…there isn't.

Except with Brady, and that's why I keep fucking him – he keeps it simple and I know he doesn't want more. He wants to fuck and that's it. He doesn't call or bother me unless it's for this. He gestures me to him and I crawl over his body, stopping to drag my tongue up his balls and along his hard cock, then slowly I taste every ridge of his six-pack. I glance up at him when he snakes his hand into the cup of my bra grabbing a mound of my full breast, finding the nipple and pinching it hard. The sensation causes me to moan and I go down on him, wrapping my lips around the head of his cock and twisting my hand with each movement. He sits up and unclasps my bra with one hand, allowing it to fall down my arms. I let go of him and he helps me take it all the way off, but my movements never falter or stop. I love getting him close; sucking him so well that he wants to come. "Fuck, Arion, I love your lips," he murmurs. I can't help but smirk. Brady takes his hands and lifts my body, twisting me so I'm now straddling his face. I stop sucking him and laugh out loud when he nips my underwear. The alcohol is beginning to make everything spin as we are now in the sixty-nine position. "Brady," I screech, as his fingers slide beneath the thin fabric of my thong, shredding it to pieces, then he tosses them across the room.

Although the act caught me off guard, it shouldn't have. This isn't the first time that he has done this and I'm sure it won't be the last. "You like it," he chuckles, wrapping his warm lips around my clit.

I whimper from the sensation and stop sucking him, enjoying the pleasure too much to do anything else. My body tingles and warms. That is, until he suddenly stops, pulls away, and sinks two wet fingers deep inside of me. Fuck, this man knows what I like way too well. *This might have to be our last time.*

As he begins to move his fingers inside of me, in and out, in and out, I focus on the pleasure to keep my mind from drifting. There's no good reason to end things with Brady, he gives me what I want, nothing more. I can't let my own insecurities from the past creep in. "Suck me," he orders.

I do so right away and get lost with Brady like we've done so many times and do so well together. I can't help my hips as they have a mind of their own and begin bobbing on his fingers. I want to fuck him. I want more. "Fuck," he groans, "You're gonna make me come."

We both stop with those words and in the flash of a second his hard cock is inside of me. "Mmmm, you're so wet."

I moan and brace my weight behind me on his hard stomach with my fingers dug into his six-pack. He's underneath me, my back is to his front, and his fingers dig deep into my skin. "I'm gonna fuck you hard, Arion."

"Fuck me," I confirm, throwing my head back, balancing above him. As he begins, everything inside of me shakes, my breasts bounce and move, and all I can do is hang on. I try my best to stay quiet, because I know there's a ton of other people in the house, but I can't.

The pleasure is too great and *fuck*, Brady is too damn

good. I clamp my pussy tightly around his cock, letting my body shudder. "Fuckkkkk," I whimper.

Brady grunts loudly, holding me up, fucking me so hard that I'm lost. Lost in this moment and in these sensations. Doing what I do best. With my eyes tightly closed, the pain of my life all washes away. In its place is pleasure, so abundant that I never want it to end.

Finally, I let go after him fucking me senseless and holding onto my orgasm for as long as I can bear to. Squeezing his dick with all of my might, I allow the world's greatest pleasure to roll through me. Then his movements slow and I look back at him. He pulls me down on top of him and wraps his arms around me, still moving slowly inside of me. "Why didn't you come?" I ask bewildered.

"I did, a long time ago."

I smile wondering how he could stay hard for so long. "Stay the night with me?" he asks, massaging my breasts.

His words are like a fire alarm and I can't get off of him fast enough. I begin getting dressed, knowing that this is the end for us.

"Come on, A, please?"

"NO! Brady, you know the rules."

"I don't care about your rules anymore. Don't you feel—"

I put my hand up to stop him, not wanting to know what he has to say. I look back at him as he clambers into his pants and bounces after me.

"Wait, Arion. Please."

But I can't and walk out of his room, slamming the door in his face. I have to leave. On the way out, I grab my coat and phone out of the kitchen and bolt through the side door, slinking away in the cold, black darkness of the night. Brady calls my name from behind me, but I don't stop. I've done this too many times to count.

I wake to the faint sound of my phone ringing. I try to ignore it, then reality smacks me in the face. *Fuck, I have work this morning.* The thought alone shoots me out of bed. I search around my room for it and just when I find it…it stops.

Sitting back down on my bed, I scroll through the call log. It was Sasha, one of the girls I work with. *Dammit!* Quickly I jump into my work clothes and then call her back. Her phone goes to voicemail and then a voice mail chimes in.

"Hey, girl, I'm sorry, but I overslept and am running a bit late. I'll be there as soon as I can. I hope you got the store open okay and it's not too busy."

Fuck. Fuck. Fuck. I fly out of my apartment and hop into my car, driving as fast as I can. Since it's five in the morning, there are barely any cars on the roads and I push the speed limit. Goddamn Brady for making me drink so much last night. I was fine 'til I left his place, then the mind-fuck began, and I had one too many drinks at home. Beating myself up, worrying about the what-ifs.

It's not long 'til I pull up to the newly built Starbucks that I manage. I've worked my ass off to get this job and I truly love it. Some might say it's not much, but to me it's the world. I wasn't fortunate enough to go to college, so I'm proud to be in the position I'm in, especially at the age of twenty-three.

Thankfully, there is only one car waiting in the parking lot, and it's Roger, one of our regulars. I smile and wave to him as I run by and unlock the door. Then I make quick work of the opening process, turning off the alarms, and powering up the place, from the lights to the machines, everything has to be brought to life.

As I get my headset on and ready for any cars coming through the drive through, Jason comes in with Roger and they are both laughing. "Morning, A," he says as he breezes by me. "Where do you want me?"

I smile looking up at him and take two gallons of milk out of the cooler. Then start to brew our daily roasts. Jason is about my age, tall with messy, brown hair and works his ass off. Well most of the time. We have fun here, that's one of the reasons why I love my job so much. "It's up to you. Sasha's late, so you can have your pick."

"Hell yeah, drive through," he says.

I can't help, but laugh at him. I know with my headset on, I'll have to listen to him joke and make customers laugh all day. But that's the job of the manager. Just then

Roger emerges from the restroom. "Good morning. How's the beautiful Arion this morning?" he asks with a warm smile spread across his face.

"I'm tired," I respond, holding back a yawn.

"Late night?" Jason asks me, handing me Roger's coffee.

"You could say that."

Our attention is diverted to Sasha as she comes through the front door with her massive mound of brown hair piled atop her head. Even running late, she's gorgeous. My hair, on the other hand, is stringy. I pulled it back into a ponytail on the drive.

"Morning," she says. "Arion, I'm sorry that I'm late. I'm so sorry."

"It's fine, it happens." I can't really come down on her considering that I wasn't on time myself. "Let's have a good day, guys," I say as the first customer chimes in on the drive through and another walks through the front door. Roger goes to pay me, and I politely hand him back his twenty-dollar bill. He always over-tips us, so the least I can do is take care of his drink this morning. My gesture backfires, as he takes the whole twenty and leaves it in our tip jar. Before I can tell him to keep it, he is walking away and I am faced with another rich New Jersey customer. Work keeps me busy for a good part of the morning and once it finally dies down, I step outside to take a break, enjoying the cold chill on my skin. I check my cell phone and notice a missed call from my roommate, Aubrey. I dial her back, and light a cigarette. *God, I really need to quit smoking*. Isn't that what all smokers say?

"Hey, girl," she answers in a bright tone.

"Hey, sorry I missed your call, works been a B."

"No problem. How are you feeling?"

I laugh, exhaling a puff of smoke. "Uhhh, I'm hanging, but I'll get over it. How 'bout you?"

"I'm good. I drank my hangover remedy and feel like a million bucks."

"You bitch, you should've made me some."

She snorts and says, "Hah, yeah right. You leave at the ass crack of dawn."

"Whatever, that's no excuse."

"So Brady, you really gonna break it off with him?"

"Aubrey, there is nothing to break off. We fuck and that's it. I told him no feelings and he's been pushing it. So I just won't answer his calls anymore when he wants to fuck."

"Hmmmm, we'll see how long it lasts. Wanna go out tonight and see what trouble we can get into?"

"If you're driving, then yes."

"Fuck no. I picked you up last night. You drive."

"Fine, I'll drive. But I get to pick where we go."

"Deal. See yah later, whore."

Laughing at her comment, I hang up and lean back against the rough brick of the building. A shiver courses through me, and for the first time since I came out here, I feel cold. *Stay the night with me?* Brady's words ring in my head like he's right here speaking them.

I wish I didn't have these problems or fears, but I do. Ever since Nate died, I've changed. There's no point in fighting them. This is the person I've become, and I have to learn to accept that. He was my everything and my future. Unfortunately, he was taken from this earth earlier than he should've been. I know what we had was once in a lifetime. Well, at least I know you don't get two soul mates anyways, so I've learned to cope the only way I know how, by satisfying the need within. If I can feed my need for sex and keep my emotions out of it while doing so, then this is the best I'll ever have.

Dropping my cigarette to the ground, I step on the remnants and head back in. Things are slow, so I work on the next week's schedule before I get the bank deposit ready. It doesn't take me long to get everything done. Before I leave, I check in with Sasha. "Hey, girl, do you mind if I run to the bank real quick?"

"Nope, go right on ahead." I smile gathering everything I need, then remove my apron. I go to head back into the office, but Jason calls me over to him.

"What's up?" I ask.

Covering his microphone, he whispers, "There's some chick in the drive through that's pissed that we're all out of croissants."

"Did you offer her one of the new chocolate-filled ones?" He shakes his head. "Then do it."

I glance outside before leaving, waiting to make sure

that he doesn't need me. The sun is peeking through the clouds, which is deceiving to say the least. I know it's not hot today.

Jason turns to me with a thumbs-up, and I grab my coat.

CHAPTER 3

-Kinsey's last days-

Are you still coming home for Mom's birthday?

I text my brother, Bain, as I try and decide what to wear to class. It's snowing like a bitch so I know it needs to be something warm. Looking through item after item, I decide on leggings with a big, tan sweater and my favorite Ugg boots. Pulling my brown hair into a low ponytail, I apply a thin layer of lip-gloss. Then I head downstairs to grab a bite to eat on my way out, and my phone vibrates just as I enter the kitchen. It's my brother, of course.

We have our last game on Friday before break. Then I'll hit the road.

"Good morning, honey," my dad says kissing me on the cheek. "Who are you texting?"

"It's Bain."

"Tell my son I love him," my mom chimes in.

22

"I will, Mom."

"What do you two feel like for breakfast?"

"I'm just gonna grab a granola bar, Mom, I'm not hungry."

"That's nonsense. You are going to eat with your father and I, like we do every day."

I roll my eyes. Jesus, she's so controlling. "Fine. I'll eat whatever you're making.

"How do blueberry pancakes sound?"

"My favorite," my dad says, and I sit next to him at the bar. "Are things still set for Bain to come home?" he asks me whispering.

I nod my head and hand him my phone, showing him Bain's last text. My mom is going to go through the roof when we surprise her.

CHAPTER 4

-Bain-

I'm not sure how I'm going to get through this dinner without any pills, but I need to be able to have a conversation that I remember and to be as alert as possible. My coach is very perceptive and I know he'll see right through my bullshit. Hopefully a strong ass Americano will sober me up enough to be able to pull my shit together.

He called and said some NBA scouts were coming to visit the university for a game against one of our big rivals. He really wants me to be there, meaning he wants me to play. I've been waiting for this day all of my life – my dreams of playing in the NBA have always been my drive. But since losing Kinsey, I just don't have the fire anymore.

"Eight fifty-seven," the cashier requests.

I hand him a twenty and wait for my drinks.

"What's up, Dad?" I answer my phone, grabbing the change back.

"Bain, are you almost home? I really need some help with your mom."

"Yeah, I'll be there soon. Is everything okay?"

"She's pissed that I won't let her drink."

"Jesus," I mutter. "I'll calm her down. Sorry, Dad, I'll be there in a few minutes."

"It's not your fault. See you soon."

Hanging up, I focus on getting home. Inside I'm nervous – nervous to see my coach and having to face him when I have no drive or ambition to return to school. Now, my mom pulls this shit. It's the last thing I need. I really couldn't care less about graduating and I can't believe I'm about to say this, but I don't think I want to play in the NBA anymore either. Since I've been out of school, I'm sure my chances of getting drafted in the first round are gone.

Also, I would have to stop self-medicating and right now I just can't. They are my lifeline and give me the only release from this excruciating pain, and quite frankly, the only things that get me out of bed every day. Pulling into the driveway, I check the time and notice that I have a little under an hour before my coach arrives. Upon entering the house, my mom is screaming; I can hear her loud and clear.

"Please, Renee, don't do this. Think about Bain."

"Fuck you, Jack," she slurs, and I know right away what's going on. Her back is to me and she's walking away from him with a bottle of vodka clutched tightly in her grip. Setting our Starbucks down, I sprint over to her and rip the bottle away. She turns to me with venom in her eyes and a snarl across her face.

"How dare you?"

"Don't, Mom," I snap as I pour the foul liquid down the sink. The moment the first splash hits the drain, she lunges herself at me and my dad grabs her.

"Calm down," he pleads, but she thrashes in his arms.

Once I have the bottle empty, I step towards them and tightly hold her face, forcing her to make eye contact with me. "You can either pull your shit together, for me, or we can do this without you!" She stares back at me stunned, completely shocked by my words. "Believe it or not, Mom, Dad and I can handle things tonight with or without you. I just thought we could still present ourselves as a family since losing Kinsey, but apparently not. I guess Dad and I are the only ones with the strength anymore."

Tears well in her eyes and I can see the despair as she looks at me. For months, she has stumbled around this house, neither of us asking her to do a thing 'til now, and the one time I need her – she can't. Christ, it makes me angry. "Don't cry. That shit doesn't work on me. If you forgot, I lost her too, Mom. It hurts just as much for me every day." Letting go of her, my father drops his arms at the same time. She stares at me with that blank, empty expression, the one she's worn since the day we first got the call. I walk off, leaving them both standing there and head to Kinsey's room. I know my mom won't come in there and bother me.

As I open the door, the scent hits me hard like it

always does, immediately taking me back to when she was alive. I flop down on her teal comforter, letting the exhaustion soak me into the mattress. *I need a pill. Fuck, I need them.* But I know I can't, so instead I focus on keeping my emotions in check. I always used to come in here while she was getting ready. I can hear her words now…

"Why do you have to flop on my bed like that?"

I shrug my shoulders, nuzzling the pillow. "'Cause I'm used to sleeping on a cardboard piece of shit box at school, Kins. This is so much better."

She laughs. "Then go and sleep on your own bed."

"What? You don't miss your brother?" I tease.

"You know I do. That's why I don't understand why you won't come home and just go to school around here, like I do."

I open my eyes and watch her apply her makeup. "I've told you before, UConn is one of the best schools when it comes to ball."

"So you really want to play in the NBA?" she asks lying down next to me. I look at her long, brown hair, and close my eyes imagining how great my life is going to be before I answer. "Absolutely, I fucking do! More than anything in this world."

She smiles turning to me. "I know it'll happen and I'll be your number one fan, cheering you on all along. You can always count on me to be at every game…"

"How are you holding up?" my father asks me, patting my back. His touch brings me back to the present – to reality.

"Fine. How's Mom?"

"I'm not sure. She locked herself in our room. So what

are you planning on telling Coach Daniels?"

"I don't know, Dad."

"Well, how do you feel about things?"

"I'm just done faking like I care about basketball. That was who I used to be. I guess I'll be honest and tell him that I'm done with ball. I have enough credits to graduate, so I'm not worried about that. I just don't have the ambition anymore. I honestly don't even think I could make a basket if I tried."

"Come on, son. You're the leading rebounder and scorer on your team. You know that your talent is natural and God-given. It's not something you've learned or been taught. It's just what you were born with. Since you could bounce the ball, you could drain shots."

I sit up off of my sister's bed and know what my dad wants. He wants me to go back to school. He wants me to graduate with the rest of my class and get drafted into the NBA. He wants me to go back to everyday life like he has. Well, I can't. We all can't move on like he has. I don't know how he does it, but he does. It's not that I resent my dad. It's just he copes with things differently than I do, therefore I don't think he can really relate to the pain that I'm feeling.

"I hear you, Dad, I really do. But…I don't think I'll ever be able to play with the passion I once had. It died the day Kinsey did."

Nodding his head, the look of disappointment is as prevalent as ever. Then the doorbell rings. He stands and says, "I'll let him in. Just come down when you're ready and please know that I support whatever decision it is that you make. You're my only son and I love you."

I nod my head. "I love you too," I respond, running my hands over my face. *You can do this. Just be fucking honest.* Before going downstairs, I stop in the bathroom and splash my face with water. God, I want to take some pills so badly, even one would take the edge off. As I emerge, I hear not only my dad, but a few of my teammates. *Fuck. Fuck! He's really bringing out all the tricks.*

Walking into the hallway, I glance at my mom's bedroom door, still shut. I'm sure she's passed out. I snag my Starbucks out of the drink holder at the bottom of the stairs and plaster on my best fake smile and *positive* attitude. "Hey, guys," I announce and everyone turns to me.

Trenton and Kohan, who are not only my teammates but also my dormmates, run over and both tackle me, almost taking me down just to give me a hug. "What's up, man? Kohan asks.

"Not much, how 'bout you guys?" I ask.

"Getting ready to impress some scouts when we play Virginia. You're gonna join us, right?" Trenton asks.

"I—"

My coach cuts me off. "Now, now, boys, we came here for dinner. Let's at least eat first before we pressure Bain into anything." We exchange a glance and it takes everything I have to hold it together. The last time I saw him was at Kinsey's funeral. "How are you?" he asks, embracing me tightly.

I don't respond, instead I just nod my head. The doorbell rings right as we separate. "That's dinner," my dad announces.

Of course he ordered in. That's all we do anymore. "How are things?" I ask him.

"Definitely not the same without you," Coach says.

"What he means is we suck!" Trenton interjects.

I chuckle at their remarks.

"We don't suck," Coach Daniels adds. "Things have just been...challenging. Enough about us and basketball, boys. How are you guys holding up?"

"We're doing the best we can, considering," my dad says taking out the containers of food and spreading them on the table. "Time has helped a bit, but the pain is still tremendous."

"Always will be," I mutter under my breath.

"I can't imagine. It's so horrible to think about what she went through," Coach says.

I stay quiet as my blood starts to boil. Why are we talking about this now? I thought this was the last direction that the conversation would have gone in.

"I can't imagine losing my little sister," Kohan says.

I shoot out of my chair and head straight to my room. Fuck being sober. I can't do this shit. As I walk away, I feel everyone's eyes on me, but I don't look back. The minute I'm in my bathroom, I open the drawer I keep my pills in and stare at the array of bottles, contemplating which to take.

I decide on a few Xanax. They have been doing me good since Jamison hooked me up, and I function well on them, plus no one will know. Although, I do love the Hydro, they really amp me up. Since my anxiety is already through the fucking roof, that's the last thing I need. Swallowing a few small, white bars, I stare at my reflection in the mirror. It's as if the person looking back at me isn't me. My eyes aren't the same; they're...empty.

CHAPTER 5

-Arion-

What have I gotten myself into? That's all that floods my mind as I leave Brady's. I caved when I saw his sexy ass at a bar last night and…fuck. I…I stayed the night with him. I haven't stayed the night with anyone since I lost Nate.

Jesus, I'm such a fucking hypocrite. All I can think about is Nate and how it feels like I've betrayed him. How did I end up in this situation? This will be the last time for sure. As soon as the thought crosses my mind, that ass texts me, *Last night was amazing. You are something else, Arion.*

A surge of nausea creeps up my throat. *Oh, what have I done?* I really hope Aubrey is home; I'm going to need her help to get him off my back. Our apartment isn't far from his and within a few minutes, I'm home.

It's early as fuck and I feel bad waking Aubrey, but I have to. Peeking into her room without knocking, I'm surprised by what I see. She's definitely not sleeping. There's someone with her in bed and they are going at it. Quietly I close the door, not letting them know I saw a thing. Undecided on how to handle Brady, I hop in the shower, hoping that will make me feel a little better.

As I wash away the guilt from last night, it still doesn't change the fact that it's done and I can't go back. As much as I'm pissed with myself, my mind stays on Nate. I miss how good it felt to be in his arms. God, when I was with him, everything was so fucking perfect. I just wish it could all go back to that. Tears gloss over my eyes and a lump forms in the back of my throat.

I know why I stayed last night. As much as I want to blame it on the alcohol, it wasn't that. I wanted to feel what I had with Nate, with Brady, but it's not there and never will be. I have to accept that I'm meant to lead a single life.

My phone vibrates again, so I decide to turn it off. My best course of action against Brady is to simply ignore him; it's what I usually do when I'm done with a guy. Crawling into my bed, exhaustion smacks me in the face…

"God, you're so beautiful," Nate says, nestled deep inside of me. Both of us are panting from the sex and the anticipation that we might get caught. We're on the beach and the sun is long gone. The only thing that lights the night sky is the moon peeking in and out of the clouds.

"I love you," I whisper.

"I love you more," he says leaving a trail of kisses down my neck, nipping and sucking along the way.

Even though his mouth is heavenly, my mind gets away from me. I need to ask him if he's heard any news. Then again, I'm terrified to know. Sometimes living in the dark is better than facing reality.

"What's wrong?" he asks knowing me so well.

"Nothing," I respond, shaking my head.

"Come on, A, I know you. Talk to me."

Swallowing hard, I look into his eyes, searching for the strength to speak. "Have you heard anything on when you're getting deployed?"

Scrunching his eyebrows, he looks at me and shakes his head. "No. Come on, A, you promised me not tonight. You said we wouldn't talk about that stuff."

"I know…it's…it's just I have to know when I'm going to lose you."

"You're never going to lose me, baby. No matter if I go or not, I'm yours," he says, taking my hand and pressing it against his chest. "Forever, you hear me?"

I nod my head, reminding myself that I have to stay positive. For us. As we watch one another, so close together and connected, I feel his dick begin to stir again. The sensation alone causes me to crash my lips to his, taking in his tongue when he seeks entrance and letting him invade my mouth.

In that moment our worlds blend together. Everything we are becomes one. I can't control the future, or what's going to happen. But what I can do is cherish him in this moment while we have each other.

Nate's movements become urgent, as does his mouth, kissing, sucking, nipping, and biting everywhere he can, matching his rhythm. The affection drives me close to climax. I moan in bliss, wrapping my legs tightly around his waist, and weave my fingers into his hair.

I hold on with everything I have, allowing him to take me on this ride. I'm so close that I drop my legs, letting my heels dig into the sand. Nate's arms hold me tightly against him, as surges of bliss rock my body.

"Let go, A," he whispers…

I wake to the reality that Nate is dead. A weight drags me down as I begin sobbing into my pillow…again. I do everything I can to stay quiet. I've dreamt that dream so many times over the last seven months, and still, I always wake when he says *Let go, A*. That night was one of the happiest of my life – I would give anything to go back.

There's a light knock on my door and before I can say a word, Aubrey enters. I turn my face into my pillow to let the tears absorb, trying to hide my pathetic outburst. She's seen me do this more times than I'd like to admit and still I'm embarrassed. "Are you ever going to wake up?" she asks me.

"What time is it?"

"It's nine."

"I just got home. I haven't even slept that long."

"Dude, it's nine at night."

I blink a few times and look at my curtains to see if there's any light shining in. She's right, it's nighttime. "Holy shit, I slept all fucking day."

"Well, I'm sure you needed it. I tried to wake you earlier but you were out cold. Did you and Brady stay up all night?"

I get out of bed and head into the bathroom, avoiding

her question. I don't want to get into things right now or admit that I stayed the night, not with how emotional I am and just waking up from that dream. We can talk about Brady later. For now, I'll avoid him.

"Who was in your bed this morning?" I ask, wanting to change the subject.

"Rodney – he's a total hottie. He wants to go out again tonight. Are you up for that?"

I glance at her for a brief second. She's sitting on the edge of my bed, her long, brown hair is curled to perfection and her makeup is already done. I can't let her down, not looking like that. Plus, I don't want to get back in that bed and risk another dream.

"Fine, give me about thirty minutes and I'll be ready, okay?"

"Cool, I'll let the guys know."

"Guys?" I question.

"Yeah, Rodney and his friends."

I smirk, shaking my head, and retreat into the bathroom. It doesn't take me but a few minutes to flat iron my hair leaving it long and down. Then I apply a little make up and head into my closet. Fuck it, I go for comfort, putting on a pair of black leggings with a soft, thin, gray, long-sleeved t-shirt and ankle boots.

Grabbing my purse, I throw on a matching beanie and pull my long, blonde hair over my shoulders. Upon entering the living room, Aubrey is in a black dress with hot pink heels. *She's so Jersey.*

"Ready?" I ask.

"Yup," she responds hopping off of one of our bar stools.

"You're driving," I remind her, shrugging my coat on.

It's not long 'til we are pulling into the lot of Pat's, a local Jersey bar. Aubrey's phone beeps with a new text message. "They're here," she responds and we head inside.

CHAPTER 6

-Kinsey-

As much as I bitch about breakfast with my parents, it's actually nice to eat with them. Plus, my mom's cooking is really the best. Thinking about some of my friends and the shitty parents they have, I really got damn lucky with mine. Hopping into my Audi, I cruise across town. College has been an experience, that's for sure.

I'm not really one of the popular girls, but everyone knows who my brother is and that makes me known. It's not a bad thing; I'm proud as hell of him. What I go through is nothing compared to what he experiences. I mean, the guy's been on TV being interviewed and playing games.

Compared to me and my simple life, I've got it easy. I love photography and go to one of the best schools for it. Plus, it lets me stay in New Jersey. Stopping at a stoplight, I text Anna, one of my good friends and also one of the smartest ones. **Hey, girl, do you have my biology homework?**

She texts right back. **Have I ever let you down, Kins?**

Very true, I do owe you. See you soon.

It's not that I don't want to do the homework. It's that I can't. Some of that shit just hasn't clicked. I don't know if I have ADD or what my problem is. The doctors say everything is fine with me, but I struggle with certain things. For me, I found it easier to pay Anna. It's really a win-win – she gets extra money which my parents have a ton of and I get my homework done.

Parking in the first spot I see, I hop out, bearing the cold weather. There's no one inside, but it is November and this winter has been brutal already. Once I'm inside, I don't waste even a second congregating or mingling with the other students, that's not me. I stick to myself heading to my first and favorite class – Photography. With my notebook in hand, I sit down waiting to see what our next assignment is going to be. Our teacher, Mr. Snell, is the best, a world-renowned photographer that's traveled the world photographing some of the most famous faces. I hope one day my dream of taking pictures for a living will come true. On the wall is a large 16x20 photo of a vacant house that I took. I can't help, but stare remembering how I took the photo from the front door looking through the house. I pressed my lens up against the glass and got a perfect view through the front room, dining room, right to the back door. I then altered the photo to look black and white and vintage. Mr. Snell loved it, too, and that's why it's on the wall. I really couldn't be happier with the outcome.

As the class waits for Mr. Snell, I realize the bell has already rung and some of the students are talking about where he is. It's not like him to be late. Then all of our attention is diverted from waiting to a young, light-haired man that walks in, stopping in front and writing his name on the board. Through his messy writing, I can *barely read the name, Anthony.*

"Sorry to keep you all waiting. My name is Anthony. If you prefer a prefix, please call me Mr. Anthony. Questions?"

Everyone including me, shakes their head staring at the gorgeous man. "I believe Mr. Snell had a family emergency, so he'll be out for a week or so, but I assure you that we'll have fun and learn a lot about each other while he is gone." As he speaks the last sentence, he looks right at me, our eyes connecting. His presence so strong, it makes my heart race a million miles a minute.

CHAPTER 7

-Bain-

"Three shots of tequila and three Coronas." Both Kohan and Trenton look at me. "What? You guys do realize that I have to pay you fuckers back for dragging me here."

"Whatever. You agreed to come. Don't be a little bitch about it."

The bartender pours our shots and we all lift our glasses, holding them high. "To the future, may it not shit on you like the past." I speak my mind like I always have and smack my shot on the bar before knocking it back.

Kohan and Trenton do the same. Then Trenton asks, "So what's next for you, are you really not going to try and play pro ball?"

"I don't know. I need to figure some shit out here. I can tell you since losing Kins, I don't have the desire to even pick up a basketball."

"That doesn't sound like you."

"It's not me, *I'm* not me. But what can I do? Life's dealt me a shitty hand of cards, a really fucking shitty one.

It's taking everything I have to just get through each day."

"Christ, man, I'm sorry," Kohan says.

"It is what it is, nothing can change it. Listen, can we not talk about how fucked up my life is for the rest of the night?" I plead, looking both of them in the eyes, hoping that they will drop it. "I just wanna forget about everything for the night."

"Deal," Trenton says. "Can we get three more shots?" he asks the bartender.

"Make it four," Kohan adds.

I look to my right and there is a cute blonde. "I can buy my own drink," she quips at him.

"Come on, girl, it's just a drink."

"I'm not your girl." I can't help, but laugh at his expression when she shakes her head. Then with a smirk on her face she turns to him and says, "It's also an invitation to converse with you." Staring him up and down she says, "I think I'll pass."

Both Trenton and I bust out laughing. She totally just dissed him. She doesn't speak another word to us, only to the bartender ordering two drinks. *Fuck, she's hot.* I'm sure she's here with someone. Regardless, I can't take my eyes off of her and I can tell my staring is making her nervous.

The bartender hands her the drinks she ordered and she turns away from me. Yet, my eyes follow her, trailing along her body. To my surprise, feelings inside of me begin to brew. She's awoken something that's been asleep for a while now, or maybe it's just the alcohol. The feelings cause my dick to harden and I pull my eyes away to keep it under control.

Fuck.

Trenton looks at me with his head tilted. "You like her?"

"Another round," I exclaim, ignoring his question. Alcohol has to help get me through this. Running my hands over my face and through my hair, I tap my third shot and knock it back. That turns to the fourth and fifth. Nothing's helping, I still can't keep my eyes off of her.

The guys have found other girls, Trenton is making out with one and Kohan is grinding the other on the dance floor. But for me, there is no one else tonight. I've been staring at the blonde all night, like a fucking stalker. She's glanced my way a few times, but that's it. Who am I kidding? I'm in no shape to be starting something with someone anyways, so I head outside for some fresh air and hope it will clear my mind 'til these fuckers are ready to leave. Leaning up against the rough, brick wall, I inhale the crisp air and close my eyes 'til the spark of a lighter clicks next to me. I turn to look and standing next to me, leaning against the brick, is the hottie from inside.

I don't know what to say, we both just stand in silence. *I should say something. Fuck, what should I say?*

"So are you really going to eye fuck me all night without introducing yourself?"

What the fuck? I swallow hard, her words catching me off guard. "Uhh, I'm Bain."

Those are the only words that come out; my heart is pounding. She laughs at me and I turn to her and ask, "What's so funny?"

"You. That's all you're going to say? *Uhh, I'm Bain?*"

"Yeah."

"Okay," she responds is a quieter tone, understanding that I'm serious. "Well, Bain, I'm Arion. I just thought with the way you've been staring at me all night, you'd have more to say."

Fuck, she's quick with words. Unfortunately for me, I'm at a great disadvantage; the bars mixed with the alcohol have made my mind fuzzy. I can't keep up with her, not like this. I need to be sober. "Was I that obvious?" I finally ask.

"Yeah."

She flicks her cigarette into the parking lot and stares at me. Pulling my eyes from the ground, I meet hers. She's gorgeous, she's really something else, I tell yah. Especially her eyes, gray and...laced with hurt, just like mine. She acts tough, but she's hiding something. "Listen, Bain, I don't know what's wrong with you."

"Nothing's wrong," I retort. "I'm...I'm just...drunk."

"Me too," she responds running her hands down my chest and pushing me harder into the wall. Our eyes never leave one another's. My breathing increases and I focus on staying calm while feeling what she is doing to me with her hands. It doesn't take but a few seconds 'til she slides them under my shirt. I may not have words when it comes to her, but my lips don't let me down. Staring into her eyes, she looks at me with uncertainty. I attempt to ease that, with a kiss.

Her lips are plump and tender. She tastes of mint with a hint of Jäger. The moment she touches her tongue with mine, my senses flip and that need that's been knocking to escape all night erupts.

A couple exits the bar and we separate for a brief moment. Then I pull her down the side of the building. The moment we are tucked nicely into the dark alley, we pick right back up. *This is seedy as fuck.*

It's a crisp night, but being with her in the cold doesn't bother me. Her hands are warm as they explore every part of my body. But being a man, I want more. "Keep touching me," I command, wanting to feel her warm hands on my cock. Holding her face, I continue to kiss her, loving the release I get while indulging in her.

"Mmmmm, you do speak."

Growling, I flip her around, now pressing her against the wall. "I do. Fuck, Arion…" I trail off, unsure of what to say next.

She makes quick work of the button and zipper of my pants and wastes no time going in, clenching me hard, just like I wanted. "Mmmmmhhhhh," I groan as she begins to stroke me.

"Your cock is big and I want it deep in my throat." She drops to her knees and I lean my hands against the wall, questioning what we are doing for half a second.

There is no one around us and no one in sight – fuck it. Her tongue hits me swirling over the end; I brush her hair out of her face and watch as she engulfs me. From tip to base, she takes me all the way. When I don't think she can go any further, she does, and her nose touches my skin. It takes real skill to take all of me. She stares up working my cock in and out of those sweet, plump lips. We watch one another, and I wonder who in the world she is. So confident, sexy, and...dominant. Christ, it's such a fucking turn-on.

Each pull and push she matches with her hand, twirling her tongue as she goes. I especially like watching her mouth stretch. Stopping for a moment, she removes her lips but jerks my shaft, quickly. "Will you come in my mouth, Bain?"

"Suck me hard and I will."

I nod my head when she obeys and feel my balls tighten. Fuck, it's been too long. Looking at her as she takes my release, her eyes are closed and she's in a zone, enjoying this. As she pushes me to orgasm, her mouth is so warm. Her movements are perfect and I come so hard in the back of her throat, pumping my hips and thrusting out every last drop of cum. To my surprise, she swallows, smirking at me the moment she finally takes my cock out of her mouth. Standing, she licks her lips. I'm panting, trying to catch my breath as she says, "It was a pleasure to meet you, Bain," and walks away.

CHAPTER 8

-Kinsey-

"Thank you so much for my homework," I tell Anna as we leave Biology and head to lunch.

"Anything for you, you know that."

"Thanks," I say checking my phone, noticing I missed a call from my brother earlier.

"Who's that?"

"Bain."

"Oh God, I was just daydreaming about him. When will I see him again?"

"Anna," I scold her. She and Bain hooked up once, in high school, and she hasn't let it go. But it's not just Anna — I think that goes for the entire female population. It's why Bain doesn't date much. When he does, women are on him, all clingy and annoying.

"What?" she asks innocently, grabbing a pre-packaged salad for lunch.

I take a tuna sandwich and buy Anna her salad like I always do for helping me out. We find a table and I stare outside, wishing it *were warm enough to eat in the sun. But that's not going to happen for quite a few months.*

"So what are you up to this weekend?" Anna asks me.

"Just getting ready for Bain to come home for my mom's fiftieth birthday."

"Do you need any help getting things together?"

Before I can answer her, we're both sidetracked by Anthony as he crosses in front of us in the lunchroom. "Who's that?" she asks.

"Anthony, he's my photography substitute."

"Dammit, I knew I should have taken photography," she whines.

I can't help, but bust out laughing. My outburst causes Anthony to look in our direction. Then it happens again, the moment we lock eyes — combustion. Pure unadulterated, carnal, sexual tension like nothing I've ever experienced.

I give him a tiny smile, it's all I can muster, staring at him like he's on a white horse, and he winks at me in return. Jesus, the guy's got to be only in his twenties, which is not far from me, but he's my teacher.

"What was that about?"

"I could ask myself the same thing, Anna."

CHAPTER 3

-*Arion*-

"Are you seriously not going to tell me where you were?" Aubrey asks, removing her hot pink heels.

"Dude, I told you. I went outside to smoke."

"A, that's bullshit. I looked for you."

"Aubrey, you're drunk."

"Whatever," she slurs grabbing a jar of peanut butter out of the kitchen cabinet.

"I can't watch you eat that shit like that; it's fucking gross. I'm going to bed," I respond and give her a hug.

"Fine, but I know you're keeping something from me," she yells as I close my door.

I'm hoping she's drunk enough to forget about things by the morning. The fucking alcohol has me spinning and I'm fighting to remove my clothes, so I just plop down onto the cool fabric of my comforter for just a few minutes and close my eyes.

Jesus, I'm such a slut. I can picture Bain standing in the dark alley with his dick hanging out watching me walk off.

That was cold. Why do I do shit like that? I'm kind of wishing I'd handled it differently; he was really sweet. But it's not me anymore. I'm fucked up. The past has screwed me over royally. Slowly, exhaustion takes me away to my paradise...

Biting my bottom lip, I shake my head fighting the feeling, wanting to hold on to this forever. But I can't. Nate knows just how to push me – I let go. Enjoying the ecstasy that crashes through me while I cry out his name, he does the same, grunting like an animal, coming inside of me.

Just as he slows, I peck his lips and hear a group of people coming towards the water. He scrambles off of me, pulling his pants up. I giggle and pull my dress down, searching for my shoes. "Just leave 'em, baby, we'll come back," he says gripping my hand and pulling me away. We run down along the water hand in hand 'til we are a safe distance away.

When we finally stop and I'm out of breath, Nate chuckles at me, looking like he's been on a nice beach stroll. "How are you not dying right now?"

"I'm a Marine, babe. I've been training for months; we run miles for breakfast."

"Well, I'm glad you're the Marine and not me," I say looking back. It looks like the group is skinny-dipping, so I guess we didn't really need to run off.

"Me too. Wanna walk for a bit?" he asks.

I nod my head, loving that we aren't in a rush to get home. Walking hand in hand is perfect. But then when I'm with Nate, everything is perfect. "Are you going to write me often?" he asks.

I glare at him. "I thought we weren't talking about this tonight."

"You brought it up first."

"Yes, I'll write you every day."

"Good, I'll write you too."

"How are your parents taking the news?" I ask.

"My dad is fine, but he's been through this himself. He served overseas. My mom on the other hand, that's a whole other story."

"I'll keep an eye on her."

"Thank you, baby." We continue walking in a content silence. "Look," Nate says as we approach a huge array of sand castles. They are all lit up and range from ships to mermaids to castles. They are so many of them.

"I didn't even know this was going on," I whisper.

"Me neither."

Both of us stare in amazement, looking at all of the intricate creations as they stand before us.

Nate sits in the sand pulling me down with him and I nestle against his chest watching the moon glimmer on the water. I exhale loudly and close my eyes, letting the sound of his beating heart soothe me.

"A?" he says, and I can hear the underlying question in his tone.

"Uh-huh," I respond.

"What do you see for the future?"

I think of his question, wondering what it will hold. "What do **you** see for the future?" I ask, flipping the question back on him, wanting to know where his head is at.

"After I'm home from Afghanistan, I wanna spend every waking minute with you. I mean, I want to now, so I can only imagine what will happen when we are apart for so long."

"I want that too."

"What if I asked you something crazy?"

"You can ask me anything."

"Before I go, I want to make you my wife. I want to leave knowing that you're mine – forever. Will you marry me, A?"

Turning around in his hold, the look of sincerity is as apparent as ever. A warm smile spreads across his face and I know he is one hundred percent serious...

Waking up again, my eyes are wet. But finally the dream was different. I made progress. For the first time in over half a year, I made progress. I'm not sure why, maybe it's because of Bain or Brady, or just *my* mental state. But whatever it is, I'm shocked. Dreams are normally my biggest enemy; they haunt my sleep like a ghost that won't go away. Yet, I want nothing more than to relive those precious memories and get as close as I can to what I once had.

Rolling over, I check the clock on my phone. It's almost eleven and I have to be at work at noon. Getting out of bed, I stretch and head right for the coffee machine. Even though I work at Starbucks, I need my caffeine now; my body can't wait for me to get to work.

Aubrey's nowhere to be seen so I check her room, hoping to wake her lazy ass up, but it's empty. *Huh?* I wonder where she is? Heading back to the kitchen, I get my fix from the Keurig and grab my phone out of my room to text her.

Where did you sneak off to?

The gym. I tried to wake you up, but again, you were dead to the world and mumbling some crazy ass shit.

I can't help, but laugh. I do sleep pretty damn hard, especially when I dream like that. With my coffee in hand I venture back to my room to get dressed for the day.

I normally go in to work without make-up, because truly, I don't give a shit what I look like when I'm there. I'm not going to pick up any elders or businessmen, that's just not my flavor. So I figure, why waste my time?

Checking the clock before I leave, I have just enough time to stop by Nate's parents' and see our dog. Since this apartment won't let us have pets and it's the only place we could afford in a decent part of town, I had to ask Barb and Jeff to take care of Zeus. It's been working out so far.

On the drive over, I call Barb. "Hey, how are you guys doing?" I ask when she answers in her sweet tone.

"Oh, hi, darling, I was hoping you'd call today. We're all right. Are you coming over?"

"Yeah, is that okay?"

"It's perfect. Do you want some lunch?"

A smile automatically breaks out on my face, "I just woke up; I'm trying to get my coffee down."

"Are you still having a hard time keeping food down?" she asks.

"No, that's a lot better. It was just a late night and I'm a little slow moving this morning."

"I'll make you some toast then. See you soon."

I hang up. Barb has been like a mother to me since the day we met. I lock up and head out into the crisp spring morning; the birds are out and I know that summer is just around the corner. It only takes about ten minutes 'til I'm at their house.

Although I know he's not here, I can still picture Nate greeting me out front. Today it's Jeff, with his dark brown hair and matching eyes. Behind him is Zeus, bouncing from the screen door to the front window, with a huge smile on his face. I swear that dog thinks he's half-human. Walking up to Jeff, I take deep breaths. Hugging him is always the hardest.

"How are you today?" he asks. "You look good."

"I am, thanks for asking. A little tired, but it'll pass."

Zeus begins to bark, causing both of us to look in his direction. "Come on, let's go in, someone misses you."

Barb greets us at the door as well and I get about half of a hug in before my pants are practically torn. "Okay. Okay," I respond leaning down to pet my pup. We head into the living room and I assume my usual position on the floor. Grabbing Zeus's face, I look into his orange eyes. My touch still calms him, making him relax as he looks back at me.

"I wish we had that power over him," Jeff says. "Because it doesn't matter what we do, he just goes and goes a million miles a minute."

"Are you hyper?" I ask Zeus. He barks at me and I tell him, "Go get your ball."

He runs off bringing me his favorite blue, rubber ball that Nate bought for him and drops it in my lap. I remember Nate picking it out and the thought sinks my stomach. I toss it down the hallway hoping it will burn some of his energy.

"Here's your toast," Barb says, coming back into the living room.

"Thank you. So how have you both been? I hope Zeus hasn't been too bad for you guys."

"He's fine, dear. I've been telling you that," she says, sitting next to Jeff on their brown, leather sofa. I lost my virginity on that couch and I'll never forget the day it happened...

"Are you sure your parents aren't going to be home for a while?" I ask Nate breathlessly as I'm pinned underneath him on his couch.

"Yeah, I promise. They are at a function for my mom's work. We have all the time in the world," he responds sliding his hand inside of my panties. Nate and I have done this so many times I can't count, but tonight I want to take it a step further.

Reaching down I remove my pants, showing him that I'm ready.

He looks up at me with a surprised expression and asks, "Are you sure?"

I nod my head, loving how his lips feel on my neck and...

"I was joking about Zeus," Jeff says interrupting my

daydream. "When you're not here, he's lazy and—"

Barb cuts him off, "Depressed. But he's fine. I've been walking him and he seems to like that. He especially loves the rain. The other day, I had to apologize to one of the neighbors because he stopped in their yard and was rolling all over their wet grass."

I laugh out loud and clamp my hand over my mouth because the tone is so loud. "That's gross, buddy," I tell Zeus scratching the top of his head.

"How's work been?" Jeff asks.

"Uhhh, it's been good, busy," I respond. "I think I've got the whole manager thing down and our sales have been really good, so my District Manager's happy."

"That's good. What about Aubrey, how is she?"

"Oh, you know how she is. She's as crazy as ever. She seems to be in a really good place though. She loves her job and there's a lot of potential there. Enough about Aubrey and I. How are you two?"

Both Barb and Jeff look at each other. "Things are okay. We both started counseling and it's helping." They look at me and I know exactly where this is going. I won't be rude to Jeff or Barb – they are like parents to me – but counseling is not something for me and that's all there is to it. There's no point for me to talk about my problems. Nothing is going to bring Nate back, no matter what. Reality is reality. There are no magic words a psychologist can tell me to help with the pain. I have my own way of dealing with things. Some might not agree, but for me it's all I've got.

I swear if I have to say "Welcome to Starbucks" one more time, I'm going to pull my hair out. Glancing at the clock, I've been here for almost six hours with no break, no food, and not one goddamn cigarette.

I don't know why, but for some God unknown reason it's been crazy busy. I keep glancing at the front door because I know Jason will be here any minute. It feels like forever and customer after customer after customer 'til he finally arrives. *Thank God.*

"Hey, how are—"

I cut him off before he can finish his sentence. "I gotta take a break before I can answer that question."

He smirks at me. I walk away and hear both him and Sasha laughing at me. I want to tell them to get to work, because my nerves are shot and I'm fucking starving, but once I emerge outside, it's bright and surprisingly warm, and the sun on my skin calms me. I take a seat on the curb next to the building and light a cigarette, inhaling the first drag as deep as I can, holding it before I exhale. Leaning back, I close my eyes. My thoughts are blank – dark. There's nothing to them and that's the way I like it.

That is 'til I sense someone staring at me. Opening my eyes, the sun shines in my face, blocking the person looking down on me. All I can see is an outline.

"You should stop smoking," he says.

The voice sounds familiar and as he moves, I recognize him right away. It's Bain. He sits next to me, touching my side. My heart begins to race at the closeness and I feel clammy. Suddenly I become a little mortified for what I did last night and just stare at him goggle-eyed. *Jesus, he's fucking gorgeous*. Like, drop-dead, make-a-girl-lose-her-words gorgeous.

"How are you?" he asks.

I shrug my shoulders, resting my head in my hand and lean forward.

"Really? That good?" he asks.

Nodding my head I glance at him, he narrows his eyes at me. "So now you're the one that's at a loss for words. How's it feel?"

"I'm...I'm not...I just didn't expect to see you here, that's all." Finally I settle on that statement wondering what the hell is wrong with me.

"Well, you just stole my words. I was shocked when I pulled up and saw you sitting here," he says rubbing the back of his neck leaning down. "So this is where you work?"

Again, I nod my head. Not really understanding why he has this effect on me. His presence shuts me down, which is not like me. I mean, last night I was the one in control.

"Seriously, Arion? Where's that mouth of yours?"

"It's here," I whisper.

"Talk to me."

I contemplate how to handle this. I should push him away and tell him to fuck off. He's stirring something inside of me that I've kept hidden for a long time. Looking at him, my stomach flutters like it did with Nate. It makes me feel disloyal, because my heart beats like it used to when he was around. Last night when I was drunk, I felt none of this, then today it hits me like a ton of bricks. Out of nowhere, the words expel themselves from my mouth of their own accord, "I'm not looking for a relationship."

"Whoa, don't get ahead of yourself, girl. Who said anything about a relationship? You act like that's what I want."

His words cut through me, but we are ultimately on the same page, which is what I want. The door behind us opens and Sasha pokes her head out. "Oh, sorry to bug you, Arion, but the stupid espresso machine is broken again. Could you fix it?"

I stand to head in and look down at Bain, sitting on the sidewalk looking up at me. I know I should just walk away, or say good-bye...but I can't. "You coming in?" I ask him.

Giving me a sly smile, he stands up now looking down at me and says, "You were taller last night."

"How would you know? I was on my knees," I tease him and walk to the struggling espresso machine.

CHAPTER 10

-Bain-

What is it with this chick? Within five minutes of being around her, my dick is at half-mast and I have to think about basketball to keep it under control. This is something I've never had to deal with.

Standing inside of the Starbucks, I watch her interact with the employees and I can tell she's the manager. I have to give her props for being able to work hard and move her way up at such a mundane job. I mean, don't get me wrong, I don't find anything wrong with her working here. In fact, it intrigues me. Well, everything about her intrigues me.

Watching her, I sit in an open chair trying not to let my mind drift. That's 'til she bends over, and fuck – I lose it. There goes all my control, everything I've been working at. My cock grows as my thoughts turn to more. Staring right at her sexy body, I can almost envision what she looks like: nude, apple ass, and great legs. I can't help, but automatically imagine myself deep inside of her. God, what

60

I'd give to bend her over and bury my cock, fucking her with deep, long, slow thrusts, giving her all of me.

She looks at me, interrupting my daydream and I turn my back, embarrassed. I should fucking leave, but I can't. What my mind and body are saying are two totally different things. To hide my humiliation, I head for the restroom with as much speed as I can, trying not to look awkward. *Fuck, it's locked.* I wait patiently, although it's not an easy task. *My fucking cock is hard.* Taking my hands, I stick them in my pockets and readjust myself. Finally, the douchebag comes out and I sneak in, exhaling deeply and splashing my face with water.

Lying on my bed, my gaze is drawn to the side of the Starbucks cup where Arion wrote her phone number, followed by a tiny heart. It took me a few minutes to pull my shit together at her work today before I could face her and I'm glad I did. Man, is that girl something else. Here I was, wondering if I should ask her for her number or not, and she just gives it to me. As I concentrate on her handwriting, I can't help but think about how nice it feels to think of something other than Kinsey for a few minutes. Recently, Kinsey's death is all that has consumed me. I let my dreams of the NBA fucking wither away. I've basically pushed away all of my friends and the life I once lived.

My eyes feel heavy as I take long blinks, enjoying the cool air from the ceiling fan that is beating on my back. I feel at peace within myself. Thinking about Arion, I remember her lips, so soft and warm. I loved how she took full control and knew exactly what she wanted. *Mmm, her mouth was so tight around my cock.* I exhale, enjoying this moment.

My cell phone rings and catches me off guard. Rolling over, I glance at the screen but it's blank. Fuck, that's not my phone – *it's Kinsey's*. Shooting off of my bed, I grab it off of my dresser where it sits on the charger all the time now. The name on the screen reads "Chase." *Who's Chase?* I think to myself, but I don't falter too long and risk missing out on an opportunity like this. "Hello," I answer in a sharp tone. My blood is surging; who in the world would be calling her?

"Uhhh, is Kinsey there?"

"Who the fuck is this?" I bark back.

"Chase."

"Why the fuck are you calling this number, Chase?"

"Kins gave it to—"

I cut him off. "Don't fucking call her that," I snarl. "Now answer my goddamn question, why are you calling this number?"

"I just wanted to talk to her. It's like she fell off the face of the—"

"Dude, do you live under a motherfucking rock?"

"No, bro!"

"Well, you're sure acting like it. How do you even fucking know her?"

"I don't need to tell you shit, especially with how you're acting. If you could tell her I called I would appreciate it."

"I can't do that – she's fucking dead."

"What?" he asks, shocked. "No. No. No."

"I know. I don't want to believe it either." It pains me to have to say the next sentence, but he needs to know. He obviously hasn't got a clue what's going on. "She killed herself."

He is silent. I feel bad, but Christ, someone needed to tell him. How in the world could he not know? It's been all over the news and everything. It truthfully is mind boggling to me.

"Oh, God, are you serious?" he finally whispers.

"Yeah, man."

"I...I had no idea. I've been doing missionary work with my church. And..."

"I'm sorry, dude."

The line goes dead. He fucking hung up. Chase. Chase. I rack my brain trying to think of someone with that name that Kinsey talked about. I wonder who he was to her. I don't buy it that he's been *traveling*. He had to have known. Dammit, I should've asked more questions and not been such an asshole.

Hopping off my bed, I head into my dad's office.

"You got a second?" I ask him.

He's seated behind his huge, glass, L-shaped desk. "Of course, what's going on, son?"

"Did Kinsey ever talk about anyone named Chase?"

He twirls his pen around and around his finger, searching his brain for the name to click. "No, not that I can recall, why do you ask?"

"He just called her phone and had no clue that she was…well, that she'd passed. I find that strange, don't you?"

"Absolutely. What else did he say?"

"He said he wanted to talk to her. I tried to ask how he knew her, but he wouldn't tell me."

"You should give his name and number to Detective Eldridge."

"Fuck that. That asshole won't do shit."

"Come on, Bain, let's trust the man to do his job."

"If he was any good at it, then yes, yes, I would."

"Just give it to him. It's not going to hurt anything, am I right?"

I nod my head, not wanting to listen to my dad, but deep down I know he's right. All we have is Detective Eldridge, so I have to tell him.

"Hey, while I have you here, I wanted to talk to you about your mom."

"What now?" I grumble.

"I think we should try and do some sort of an intervention."

"Dad, she's not going to go for that. You should just forget about rehab and accept this is how she is."

"Bain, listen to yourself. This is your mom we are talking about. I can't sit back and watch her do this anymore. She's slowly killing herself. Don't you remember how she was before all of this? I know that woman is still inside of her, we just need to help her find her way out."

"Dad, I love you both and I'm sorry to say this, but I think she might be a lost cause right now."

"Fine, I'll do it without you, Bain," he says firmly. I can tell by the look in his eyes he's mad at me.

"Okay, I'm sorry. Just look into Betty Ford or a place like that and let me know what you find out. I won't let you do it alone." A small smile comes across his face; my answer has satisfied him. Walking away, I head back to my room to call that asshole detective.

CHAPTER 11

-Kinsey-

Walking into school, I'm nervous as can be and questioning my clothing already. Glancing down at my black skinny jeans and leather boots, I feel like a biker chick. What in God's name was I thinking? I mean, for real!

Before entering Photography, I stop in the restroom to calm my nerves before I face him. But truly, I don't know why I even care what Anthony thinks of me; he's my teacher and that's always a number one rule to them – never get involved with students.

Whatever, I can still look good, so I put on some powder and wash my hands. That'll do. I leave the restroom and just as I exit, fate hits me smack in the face. Staring down at me, causing me to get instantly lost in his eyes, is Anthony. I don't move or say a word. Christ, he's gorgeous.

"Hey, I was hoping I would get to see you today." I look up at him and blink a few times trying to process his words. That's all I can muster. Then the bell rings and he says, "Stay after class," before turning and walking off, not waiting for my response.

After standing there stunned, and realizing how dumb I must look, I somehow manage to walk in behind him and take my seat, getting lost in his voice. It's like silk, absolutely beautiful like he is. Watching the way he presents himself to the class is nothing I've ever seen a teacher do.

"Kinsey, would you mind coming up here?" he asks, pulling me off of the cloud I'm lounging on. I'm shocked that he knows my name, and once I yank myself out my daze, I make it to the front of the classroom.

"So, let's take Kinsey for example. When you look at her, what do you all see that you could photograph to make a unique picture?"

"Her eyes," someone from the back shouts.

Being this close to Anthony makes me nervous. He smells delicious; his voice is so strong and echoing as he commands attention from the class.

"Lips."

"Skin."

"Those are all great examples, but I want you to dig deeper. What about her hair?" He runs his fingers down the ends of it and I try to contain a shiver. "Could you zoom in as far as possible and capture what her strands really look like?"

The students nod their heads in agreement. "Will someone flip the lights off? How about now? What do you see?" The class stares at me, and the whole time I have my eyes locked on Anthony. "Or now," he says, taking a high-powered flashlight, holding my hand up and shining the light through it.

"You can photograph any human, besides yourselves. The picture needs to be no larger than a 5x7, so that's not a lot to work

with, and remember, with photography, there are absolutely NO limits. Try anything that you think will give you the perfect picture. I want something with as much detail as possible."

"Does the picture have to be recognizable as to what it is?" Sean, one of the guys in class, asks.

"I don't know, Sean, does it?"

The two men smile at each other and then Anthony directs me to take my seat. "Any other questions?" Everyone is silent. "Then class is dismissed. Go get started on your projects."

The students all look around at each other, like this guy is crazy or something. Snell would never let us out of class early. As the class filters out, I just try to keep my eyes off of him.

CHAPTER 12

-*Arion*-

"Well, you shouldn't have given him your number if it's gonna make you act like such a cunt," Aubrey teases me.

"I'm not being a cunt. I just thought he would have called by now."

"You could always call Brady," she offers.

"Fuck no. I'll wait for Bain."

"Excuse me," she exclaims, flinging around and staring at me with her flat iron clamped tightly on a strand of her long, brown hair. "What's wrong with you, A? Do I need to call a doctor?"

"No," I retort.

"Well, you've been all down in the dumps about this guy. Plus it's not like you to wait around."

"I'm not down – don't say shit like that – and I'm definitely *not* waiting around for him."

"Sure, whatever you say, girl."

"Stop it, snatch."

"Make yourself useful and pick me out something hot

to wear."

Aubrey changes the subject and I'm happy that she does. Getting off of her bed, I walk into her rainbow-colored closet that looks like the Jersey Shore threw up in it. Skimming through the items, I decide on an electric blue, skintight dress. "How's this?" I ask, walking out.

"You know me far too well, that's exactly what I was thinking."

Lying back down, I'm tired and know I won't be up long after she leaves. It makes me really thankful she's going out tonight.

"What do you think?" she asks, walking out of her closet with her hands on her hips.

"I love it. Are you going out with Rodney again?"

"Yeah, I'll probably stay at his place, too. Will you be okay here all alone?"

"I'll be fine. Text me if you need anything."

"Will do, girl," she says, as she packs her purse full of everything she'll need for the night.

After Aubrey is gone, the house is very quiet. I wonder if I should eat something or just head to bed. Staring in the empty fridge, I decide fuck it. My bed is the better option. Climbing underneath my warm covers, I'm instantly relaxed.

As soon as I close my eyes, my thoughts are filled with Bain. I'm caught off guard, as normally all I see is Nate. I can see the look in his eyes as he stood there looking down at me while I had his hard cock in my mouth. It's something I don't think I'll ever erase from my memory.

I exhale with a smirk on my face and slowly drift off. But my phone vibrates next to me, waking me before I can get into a deep sleep. I ignore it, sure it's Aubrey. Then it vibrates again. Fuck, she must be drunk already. Reaching next to me on my bed, I blink a few times and check the time. I've only been laying here for about seven minutes, when it felt like hours. I don't recognize the number, and the words are definitely not Aubrey's.

You have plans tonight?

I'd love to take you to dinner. Sorry this text has taken me a bit to get to. I've had some family shit to deal with.

I know it's Bain, but I feel like fucking with him. He did make me wait almost a week before he texted me.

Who is this?

Oh shit, sorry. It's Bain. If you're busy, I understand

Bain, why don't you cut to the chase? You wanna fuck, so there's really no need for dinner.

Maybe I wanna fuck. But I also want to take you out.

I contemplate his words. I'm not sure what to say to him, I don't like to do dinners. However, he makes my decision very easy with his next text.

Send me your address. I'll come over, maybe we'll eat or maybe we'll fuck.

I know what I should do, but for some reason, I can't say no to him. I've been waiting to see him again; he's all I've really thought about for the entire week. I text him back with my address and nothing else, then do my best to pull myself together.

I'll be there in 30, wear a dress and no panties.

I laugh out loud. **I don't wear dresses.**

You do tonight. Now you've only got 27 minutes left.

Tossing my phone on my bed, I scramble out of my room and into Aubrey's closet. She'll have something for sure. Searching through dress after dress after dress, none of them seem right, 'til I come upon one of the last ones. It's dark red with tight long sleeves and a billowing black bottom. My black ankle boots will look perfect with this. Taking it quickly into my room, I shed my pajamas and slide on the short dress, leaving all undergarments off. My hair is messy, super messy, so I decide to pull it into a low, side bun with a few locks framing my face. Then I apply a thin coat of make-up and brush my teeth before adding my lip-gloss.

There, done and done, just as there is a knock on my front door. With a stomach full of butterflies, I walk towards it, gently placing my hand on the knob. *Why am I so nervous?* He knocks again, not waiting patiently, and this time I open it. Standing before me, with a huge bouquet of flowers, is Bain. He's in a black button-down shirt and jeans, his light coat is slightly open, letting me have a good look at all of him.

"Hey," I say keeping my cool. This time, I won't let my confidence get away from me. We've agreed to no feelings and I know he knows how serious I am about that. There is no harm in spending some time with him.

"Damn, you look sexy in that dress."

"Thanks."

"You're welcome," he says pressing his lips to mine. His kiss catches me off guard. But he smells amazing...I hope he says fuck dinner. He steps inside, handing me the flowers and asks, "Do you live here alone?"

"No, I have a roommate." I put the flowers in a vase.

"Ready?" he asks and I know he means dinner, not to fuck.

I nod my head and follow him outside. Surprisingly, it's a nice night out. Well, at least it's not freezing. He grabs my hand and I look down at our intertwined fingers.

My anxiety spikes and I remind him, "Remember, no feelings."

"I heard you the other day; you don't need to say it again. I should be the one telling you not to have feelings for me. I'm pretty fucked up."

"Well, that makes two of us."

"So I know your rules. But when I'm with you, you're mine and I'll do as I please. Don't worry about me; I'm fine with things just like this. I'm not looking for anything serious."

I smile, looking into his light eyes as he opens the door to his car and ushers me in. The cool leather touches the backs of my thighs. Bain hops in the driver's seat and pulls onto the main road without any more words. "Where are we headed?" I ask.

"The city."

It's been a while since I've been to New York. "Do you live there?" I ask.

"No, I live in Jersey, about fifteen minutes from your work."

"Do you live alone?" He shakes his head, but doesn't answer my question. "Roommate?" I ask, hoping to God he's not married or living with a girlfriend or some crazy shit like that.

"If you consider my parents that, then yes."

Well, that's better than I'd thought. "What do you do for a living?"

"Nothing as of now. I was going to try and make a living playing basketball, but I just left school to handle some family stuff."

"Really?" I question.

"Yeah, but my heart's not in the game anymore. For now, I need to be with my family; that's what's important."

I wonder what in the world caused him to leave school and a shot at something so big. Maybe one of his parents is sick?

"Let's not start the night off talking about my problems. So tell me, what's your favorite food?"

Turning in my seat, I stare at him. "Really, anything."

"Anything?" he repeats after me.

"Yeah, I eat just about everything, and if I've never had it, I'll try it."

"Damn, that's about the best answer you could have given," he says, loosening his grip on the wheel as we cross over the Brooklyn Bridge.

For the rest of the drive, we keep the conversation light and enjoy some quiet time as well. I'm comfortable with Bain, more comfortable than I have been with anyone in a long time.

After an hour drive, we pull up to the valet at Damikus' and I'm shocked. I've always dreamed of coming here, but never expected someone to bring me on a first date.

"This okay?" he asks.

I nod my head in agreement, spurring him to get out of the car. Walking around, he greets the valet and then helps me out. Entering the all white eatery, it is more beautiful in person than I'd ever imagined. Bain talks to the hostess who seats us right away. The booth is small and private, shaped like a U.

The waiter comes right over and takes our drink order. I order something strong to calm my nerves – I don't belong in a place like this. Sitting next to Bain, his arms are stretched across the back of the booth, tattoos showing, and he's got not a care in the world. I can't help, but drool as he takes one of his hands and runs it through his hair.

"Why are you looking at me like that?" he asks.

"Like what?"

"Like you want me to fuck you right here, right now, on this table in front of everyone."

I didn't know I was looking at him any specific way, I was just admiring how goddamn sexy he is, but now that he mentions it, my legs are pressed together and my insides are tight. "I'm just admiring the view."

"Don't play coy with me. I know what you're thinking. Don't be afraid to say it."

Obeying his command, I lean into his neck and breathe him in, allowing his warmth to absorb into me. Then taking my teeth, I begin to nibble and suck on his rough skin, he tastes so sweet. A light growl erupts from within him and he moves his hand gripping my hip. I hold his thigh and then the waiter clears his throat, interrupting us.

"Your drinks," he says. Bain scowls at him and I pull away, but Bain stops me, holding me close to him. The waiter can tell that Bain's pissed and nods his head in apology before walking away.

His eyebrows are creased and clear frustration is written all over his whole face. "You're the one that wanted to have dinner," I say. "I would have been just fine staying at my house and fucking."

"I'm sure you would've, but now that we're here, we're going to make the best of it," he says, reaching under the table and beneath my skirt, cupping my sex. My breathing immediately becomes heavy, as he slides a finger in between my folds, touching my clit. I move my hands, bracing one of his thighs, and leave the other next to me.

"Fuck, Arion, you're so hot," he whispers into my ear.

I whimper quietly and push myself against his hand. "You want more, don't you?"

"Please," I practically beg, nodding my head.

"I'll give you more, but only if you'll come right here for me in the middle of this restaurant." I contemplate his words, then he sinks two fingers inside of me and I know what I want. The sensation is too great to fight. It's absolutely intoxicating.

While my eyes roam the sea of tables, I fight to keep them open while making sure I stay completely quiet. I wonder if anyone else knows what we're doing. Then Bain says, "Look at me, concentrate on my face as if we are having a conversation, and whatever you do, don't close your eyes when you come."

I nod my head while Bain works my pussy slowly, both inside and out. "You like this, don't you?" he questions into my ear. "You like me getting you off in public, huh?"

"Yes," I whisper.

"Mmmmmmm," he growls, kissing my neck.

My body tightens and tingles from his touch. The adrenaline alone is such a rush. Then the waiter comes by and I freeze, expecting Bain to stop, but he doesn't. He only slows the thrusts and pinches my clit, rolling it between two of his fingers.

"Do you both know what you would like tonight?"

I shake my head and Bain laughs at me, ordering for both of us. That's why he wanted to know what kind of food I liked. He had this planned all along. The waiter glances between the two of us as Bain speaks and each time he looks at me, I become nervous. Bain keeps massaging my clit, especially when the waiter looks at me. It's like he wants the guy to know what we are doing.

Finally, he turns his back and walks away. "You're so fucking hot letting me do this to you. He knew what we were doing. Did you see the way he looked at you?"

I lean my head back, unable to answer. His movements are quicker and everything inside of me is right on the edge. *Jesus, I can't believe I'm about to do this.*

"Look at me," he commands. The second I open my eyes and look into his, I lose it, coming hard with a surprisingly and unusually violent jolt to my system. Bain claims my mouth and I let my body spiral. Thankfully, our kiss quiets any noises that were about to escape. Then, my breathing slows and the realization of what I've just done, hits me as Bain says, "You're my new favorite aphrodisiac."

Jesus Christ, could this guy be any more charming? All sorts of thoughts rush through my mind as he pulls his fingers from inside of me and takes them right to his mouth, sucking off my arousal and orgasm. "Mmmmm," he says. "I think I'll skip my dinner."

Looking at him with my jaw hung open, he laughs.

"You can't be serious," I respond.

He removes his wallet and begins to pull out a hundred dollar bill. "Oh my God, Bain. You are fucking crazy."

"I know what I want, and food is not it. Let's leave, we can get a hotel and stay the whole night together."

His words change everything. *NO!* As enticing as he is and as much as he intrigues me, I can't. That's a rule I won't break again, not after the other night with Brady, I just can't. "I'm really hungry," I lie.

CHAPTER 13

-Bain-

"Fine, if you're hungry then we'll eat. I wouldn't deprive you," I say.

She smiles at me and I notice that her usual smirk and feistiness from earlier are gone. Did I say something wrong? Was getting her off, here, too much? She seemed to really enjoy it, but now she's different. The waiter comes back with new drinks, looking refreshed as if he just jerked off.

I know he knew what we were doing; I saw him staring at my hand under her dress. "Your food should be right out," he says.

"Thanks."

"I'm going to go to the restroom real quick," Arion says.

I nod my head watching her slide out of the booth. She is something else. As she moves across the restaurant, I watch just about every guy in here turn and stare at her.

I'm one of them, and it makes me want to follow her.

I try and take my mind off of her by scrolling through my phone 'til she returns.

"Hey, sorry," Arion says returning to the table.

"Don't be," I respond, setting my phone down.

"Listen, I need to be honest with you." Swallowing hard, I nod my head not liking the sound of her tone. "Bain, I like this. I like what we are doing. But…" she trails off and puts her head in her hands.

"Just say it, I can handle it."

"I can't stay the night with you, tonight or ever."

I blink a few times trying to process why. "Fuck, you have a boyfriend, don't you?"

"NO!" she counters. "It's not that at all. It's me, it's my past, and because of it, sleepovers are off limits. They complicate things and quite frankly, are more intimate."

"Why are you like this?" I ask confused. If she's that into sex, why doesn't she want to spend the night together?

"It's a really long story."

"Well, I have all the time in the world," I respond, a little annoyed.

She looks at me a little unsure and I actually feel bad for the sarcasm that was laced in my tone. "In all seriousness, you can tell me. I promise I won't judge you."

She nods her head as she begins, "I lost my fiancé about seven months ago. He's a marine." She corrects herself. "He was a marine, and after the news that he died, I just didn't know how to cope. I fell into a depression, and one night when I was drunk, had a random hook up with one of my roommate's friends. I realized then that sex could be a release, almost a way to let go and forget the pain for a little bit. Honestly, Bain, I don't normally do dinners or anything like this, but you made it impossible to say no."

"Fuck, Arion." Those are the only two words I get out. How in the world do I respond to that? Her honesty completely catches me off guard. Here I am being a complete prick, wanting to spend the night together, thinking more about myself, when she's been through hell. She is so strong, considering everything she's endured. The waiter sets down our meals and when she looks at her food, she smiles. "You like it?" I ask.

"Yes, it's perfect."

"Good. Listen, I'm sorry I was rude," I begin to say, spreading my napkin on my lap, but she cuts me off raising her hand.

"You weren't rude. I totally get that my quirks are frustrating. Fuck, I would feel the same way if I were you. I just wanted you to know that it has nothing to do with you."

"Well, I appreciate the honesty. I really do. Probably more than you realize, and I'll respect your decisions, whatever they may be."

Her smirk is back as she glances at me out of the corner of her eye. "Thank you."

"She looks good, don't you think, son?"

I nod my head answering my dad's question as we drive back from visiting my mom in Virginia. He reminds me of a little kid, hanging on to so much hope that she'll make it through this without relapsing. I myself am more of a realist and know that a high percentage of alcoholics will relapse within the first year alone. I can't imagine what that would do to him.

"You're quiet today. Is everything all right?" he asks.

"Yeah, I'm good. I'm just lost in my own head."

"It's an easy thing to do. Listen, I have a convention is Seattle this weekend. Will you be all right while I'm gone?"

"Dad, I'm twenty-two. I'll be fine."

"I know, I just worry about you."

And I know right where this is going. He's worried that I'm going to hurt myself like Kinsey did. Well, that's not me. It's not something I would ever contemplate doing.

"I'll be fine, I promise."

He looks over at me and smiles.

"Thank you."

I couldn't imagine putting him through that pain after experiencing it myself and seeing what it did to both him and my mom. Resting my head back, I close my eyes.

Then my phone vibrates and I see a new text from

Arion. I haven't heard from her since I dropped her off after dinner. I wanted to fuck her so badly that night, but I respected her wishes of no overnight visits and it was late, so I was a gentleman. Since then, I have given her some space.

You doing all right? I haven't heard from you, her text reads.

Yeah, I'm okay. Handling more family business, plus I wanted to give you a little space.

I don't need space, Bain. In fact I need the opposite.

Now I'm completely confused. How does this work? I can't have feelings, we can't stay the night together, and she's fresh off of losing her fiancé, but she wants me all up in her business?

Please clarify for me what you need, because I'm fucking confused.

I need you to not fall in love with me or ask me to spend the night with you. Apart from that, I'm down for anything. I wanna fuck. I wanna see you completely naked. I wanna feel your cock inside of me.

Are there other rules?

No.

Can we fuck other people?

If you want to, yes.

Jesus. What kind of girl says shit like that? This is something that most guys would die for. I'm not sure what to do, or how to handle her. I guess with my dad going away for the weekend, I could put the ball in her court.

I live on 118 Riverview Terrace Way; I'll have the house to myself this weekend. You're welcome to come by any time you want.

Finally, my dad pulls his Range Rover into the driveway and it's never felt so good to be home and out of the cramped quarters of a vehicle. Note to self, no more road trips for me.

"When will you be home?" I ask my dad as we walk into the house, noticing Velma, our housekeeper, cleaned it to perfection while we were gone.

"My flight gets back Monday morning. I had Velma stock the fridge so you should have everything you need here. But please—"

Cutting him off, I give him a hug to relieve some of his anxiety. "Dad, I'll be fine. I swear to God, you don't have to worry about anything. I won't put you through that pain."

He looks at me with tears in his eyes. "I'm going to go pack."

Smiling, I flop down on the sofa and still wonder to this day how in the world Kinsey could have done what she did. I mean, the way she did it was easy, but still, it's the fact that she did it at all. She had to have thought about taking her life for weeks, even months, years, and all along she was hiding it from everyone.

I just feel like there had to have been so much more bothering her, to make her go to those extremes. Something deeper – but what? If there was something, she fooled me. I've searched her room, talked to her friends, and exhausted just about every last lead imaginable. I mean, at this point, the police station should start to pay me for all the time I've put into everything.

Fuck, thinking about her and all of this shit gets me so pissed; I feel like I could lose my mind. I don't want to be mad at her, but how can I not? She tore our family to shreds. Why didn't she come to me and tell me that she was feeling that way? We were best friends. Hell, we were twins and had been together since the moment that we were born. I would've done anything for her, to help her and get her through those tough times.

What the fuck am I wasting my time for now? It's too late. She's gone and I'm not going to take myself down this path again. I've done it time and time again. It pains me that I've lost her, that she decided to leave it all. Heading to my bathroom, I pop a few pills. Letting the chalkiness dissolve on my tongue. I go back downstairs to wait for them to hit me and check my phone. Arion hasn't texted me back. I toss it next to me and flip on the TV. Right away there's a basketball game on. It's been months since I've seen any ball, so I force myself to watch it. Maybe it will give me back my drive or at least help me decide what

I'm going to do with my life. I know I can't live at home and off of my parents forever. Well, I could, but…I don't want to.

"Glad to see you're watching some ball," my dad says. "Listen, I'm gonna run so I can stop by the office on the way out to the airport."

"Sounds good, have a good time."

"Thanks." He pats my shoulder, and then he's gone.

I'm not sure how long I stay on the couch or how much of the game I even watch, the pills have me so spun. But the doorbell rings and I'm hesitant to answer it; it's always people selling shit. Then I remember I gave Arion my address, but there's no way she would show up over here without calling me. *Would she?*

Looking out the peephole on the door, I'm shocked. *Damn straight she would.* This chick is fucking crazy. Upon opening it, I'm struck by her beauty. So natural and confident, instantly my cock twitches and begins to grow, straining the fabric of my shorts. Damn thing has a mind of its own.

"Hey," I say.

"Hey. So this is really where you live?"

"Yeah, did you think I was lying?" I ask, gesturing her inside. She walks past me, looking around, and I kiss her on the cheek. *Hmm, she smells so good.* "Why didn't you call?"

"You didn't say I needed to," she responds, setting her purse down.

"True, I just assumed you would."

"When it comes to me, Bain, don't assume anything."

"That, I can do." She sits at the island and I ask, "Are you hungry?" I ask, knowing I need food to get my head leveled.

"I always am."

"Me too. Wanna eat?"

"Depends on what you're making."

I glance in the freezer, naming the first thing that I see. "I can put a pizza in the oven."

"Pizza's cool," she says looking around the house.

She seems nervous, not like herself. "Are you all right?" I ask.

"Yeah, why?"

"You just seem a little distracted."

"I just didn't expect your house to look like this."

"Well, it's not my house. It's my parents'."

"You know what I mean, this place is crazy nice. Where are they this weekend?"

"My dad is out of town on business and my mom is…" I stop myself before answering.

"Girls' weekend? Cabo? Business too?" she asks.

I shake my head and figure honesty is the way to go after she was so upfront at the restaurant. "She's in rehab."

"Oh shit Bain. I'm sorry."

"Don't be, it's better for her there right now."

Arion nods her head as if she understands.

"Want me to show you around?" I ask.

"Sure."

I pop the pizza in the oven and then reach for her hand, before leaving the kitchen. I start with the main level which is our family room, my dad's office, dining room, kitchen, and the indoor pool. I press the button, opening the automatic roof and she stares at the pool, steam dissipating off of it in the cold, spring air.

"Holy shit," she exclaims. "You can swim year round?"

"Yeah, we can as well if you're interested, later."

She turns towards me and I can see that look in her eyes. She doesn't make a move, and since I know I need to eat, neither do I. I show her the rest of the house, the basement, and then upstairs.

"What's this room?" she asks.

Shaking my head, I don't answer her question and walk off. She follows me into the kitchen and just when I pull the pizza out, she says, "Come on, Bain, you don't need to keep things from me."

"It was my sister's."

"Did she move out?"

Tilting her head to the side, she looks at me. I don't know how to say the words without breaking down. On the fridge is her memorial card and I pass it to her.

It takes Arion one glance to know right away what she's holding and a sheen of white covers her face. "Oh God, Bain. I'm so sorry. I don't know what I was thinking, coming here, into your home like this without calling you first. I can go."

"No, no, it's fine, you didn't know and I didn't know how to tell you. Trust me when I say I want you to be here, I really do. Please don't leave."

She stares down at the picture and runs her thumb over Kinsey's face. "Jesus, she was so young. Was she older or younger?"

"Younger, by about a minute and a half. We were twins."

"Shit. If I could ask, how did she die?"

"It was her decision, Arion. Listen, I don't know if I can talk about this right now."

She nods her head in understanding and places the card back on the fridge. "Jesus, life can be so fucked up."

"Can it? Or is it the people around us who make stupid ass decisions?"

She doesn't answer me and an awkward silence takes over the kitchen. I fear I've said something wrong, but sometimes, I don't know how to talk around her.

"Come on, let's eat. I know you came here for business."

She smirks at me in only the way Arion can.

CHAPTER 14

-Kinsey-

As the rest of the class floods out, I get up and pretend to head that way. Although Anthony asked me to stay after, I know I shouldn't – he's my teacher and I don't want to get him in trouble.

"Kinsey, can I see you?" he asks. I turn and see him walk towards me. "Where were you going?" he whispers.

I shrug my shoulders looking into his alluring eyes, they are the color of the sky and lighter than any I've ever seen.

"I don't want to get you in trouble."

"How could you get me in trouble? I'm allowed to ask my students to stay after class."

"Anthony, it's more than that. Maybe it's just me, but I sense a tension between us."

Taking my hand, he briefly holds it and says, "No. It's not just you. That's why I wanted you to stay. Will you have dinner with me, tonight?"

Tilting my head, I look at him quizzically. "You won't get me in trouble, I promise. I'm only here for the week, then Snell will be *back and if I don't get to know you now...Well, I'll always regret it."*

"Okay, just dinner though."

He winks at me, kissing the top of my hand, and I almost come undone. I guess it's because I've never had anyone show me attention like this. Of all the people I've been involved with, it's been purely sex. There has been no romancing to get us to home base.

CHAPTER 15

-*Arion*-

Watching Bain devour his pizza has to be one of the sexiest things ever. I mean, how do you even eat pizza and turn someone else on? It must be my dirty sex-filled mind watching his tongue and mouth, imagining the things I want him to do me.

I love how the simple things with him distract me from the reality and the pain of what I've gone through. Knowing that Bain has been through a similar loss so recently, comforts me in a way, it's like he can relate. Since losing Nate, I haven't let anyone aside from his parents and Aubrey, know what I'm really going through. But with Bain, he knows; he's been there himself.

Looking at him, my pain is replaced with a need, a need for the pleasure of something. It's something I really can't control.

He mutes the TV, which is on ESPN, and turns towards me. "Do you have a curfew?" he asks sarcastically.

I shake my head. "No, definitely not."

"Good, just checking," he says leaning over and pressing his lips to my neck. My senses awaken. His touch does that to me. Even being in close proximity to him sets me off. "Get undressed," he orders.

Swallowing hard, I push away the butterflies in the pit of my stomach and stand before him. He leans back with his arms outstretched behind him, watching me intently. The intensity in his eyes makes me nervous. It's almost like I'm going to disappoint him, which is not something I'm used to.

Lifting the hem of my white t-shirt above my head, he stares at my breasts like he's never seen them before, then I realize, he hasn't. Standing before him in just my bra and panties, he says, "The rest."

I shake my head, wanting him to do it. A devilish grin spreads across his face when he catches on to my game. He stands up and stalks towards me. I take a step back, wanting to entice him.

"Oh no, you don't," he says reaching for me, but I slip out of his grasp and make a dash for the pool. Bain is close behind me. I cannot only sense his presence, but hear his deep breathing as well. My heart pounds against my chest, the anticipation of him catching me is too great. Then the moment I'm close enough to the water, I dive in. The warm water engulfs me and when I come up for air, Bain is undressing. I watch him take off every last piece of clothing, 'til he stands before me completely naked, and sexy as sin.

His cock is fully hard and he's pissed that he couldn't get to me. I know that playing with him like this has driven him mad. He dives in and comes right to me, but I don't move. As much as I want to keep playing, I stay where I am, having him right where I want him. As he surfaces, his hands skim my body and he pulls me against him, throwing me over his shoulder so my ass is in the air. The cold air pricks my skin, but it's quickly washed away with his warm hand as he lands a firm smack. Even though I still have my underwear on, they don't protect me. The sting of the air, water, and his hand send a chill through my system.

"That's for running from me," he says. "And this is for making me wait to see you naked." Another loud noise echoes in the room and he shreds my thin lace underwear while I balance on his shoulder, then he tosses them in the water. He rubs two fingers inside of my folds, then sets me down. His touch, oh God, his touch is something else. It ignites my insides and takes everything I have to control the jolts that burn through me as he unclasps my bra. Standing before him in the shallow end of the water, he has claimed me. Two of his fingers sink deep inside of me, while his other hand has removed my bra and begins to caress my breasts.

"Fuck, your tits are perfect," he says leaning down and taking a nipple in between his soft lips, then he nips on the end. I moan in response, pulling him harder against me. "You want me to fuck you, don't you, Arion?"

"Maybe," I respond, loving how easily he is to play with. He squints his eyes and looks into mine. His are the color of the water, so light and wanting. With an act of brazenness, I reach down and clench his hard cock.

"You're a dirty girl, aren't you?" With a tiny nod, I frantically start kissing him and he walks us across the pool. I stumble a few steps, then when we reach the far edge, I wrap my arms and legs around him. He presses my back against the cold tile. Shivers take over me and only get worse when he lifts me out of the pool and sets me on the ledge.

"Open your legs," he orders.

I do so, but it's not wide enough. Bain shakes his head in displeasure and takes my feet, setting them right where he wants them, far apart. Looking down at his tattooed fingers, he holds my legs even wider and blows a breath of cold air on my clit. I squirm, but he doesn't allow me to move, holding me motionless while he takes his time dipping his tongue in between my slit.

Fuck, he's good. Leaning back, I stretch one arm above me and clench his hair with the other. I love how he does whatever he wants to me. My insides scream for a release, and with Bain, I know it won't be long 'til he gives me one.

I close my eyes, enjoying the bliss. This is one of the only places where I'm at peace. All the pain of the last seven months is gone. Everything vanishes and nothing that I've been through matters. I'm just right here in this moment. Freedom surrounds me – clear, even, deep freedom. There are no worries when I'm here. Just pleasure. Just ecstasy. Just…

Abruptly everything becomes too intense, and I moan loudly, giving the control of my body over to Bain. Without holding back my noises, he pulls away and says, "Fuck yeah; let me hear how good it feels."

He moves back into me and sinks two of his fingers deep inside, rubbing so softly. I clench tightly around them, imagining they are his cock. Stroking and working me close to climax. Being greedy, I fight coming with all that I can. 'Til finally I submit, letting my body fall against the hard cement floor.

Bain pushes against me the moment I let go. The pressure is almost too much to handle, and I lift my ass a little off the ground, countering him, pushing back just as hard. As I come violently, my noises echo around the room. The perfect combination of his fingers and tongue is too much for me to ward off and send me completely out of this world.

After my body settles, I try to tame my breathing and blink a few times, but he doesn't give me a minute. Instead, he lifts me back into the water and grabs my face with his wet hands. "I've always wanted to fuck in here," he says.

With heavy breaths, I want to give him that more than anything and reach between us. "Are you okay without a condom? I'm on birth control." I reply. He nods his head and I glide him inside of me. Water leads his cock, giving me the best sensation and right away I love having him nestled inside my pussy. Finally. It feels like we've been waiting for this moment, forever. He growls, as we stand like this, holding both my breasts, and I wrap my body around him. Our bodies fit so perfectly together. Bain looks into my eyes without moving, but I need more of him. Not wasting another second, I jive my hips, guiding myself up and down his shaft, getting the right friction, just where I need it.

Feeling what each other really feels like, he murmurs, "Fuck, you're greedy." And leaves sweet kisses on my shoulder.

"It's your cock, it's fucking amazing," I say breathlessly.

"You feel just as good. We can do this all weekend if you want."

Watching how we fuck and the way his tattooed body looks against my white skin is something else. I nod my head, agreeing to a weekend's worth of sex. I can't resist him, and I definitely want to do this all weekend. I'm not sure how he doesn't need to move more urgently. He's patient, unlike me. What I'm doing is not enough. I need more. Harder. Deeper. Rougher. I'll take anything he's willing to give as long as it's more.

"Fuck me," I command, frustrated from bucking my hips.

"You want me to fuck you?" he asks, bracing his

hands on my sides.

"Please." Finally he sinks all the way into me. Looking down, into the water, his hands grasp my skin and it's just the right amount of pain. Then he helps to guide me up and down his massive cock, meeting my movements. There's no mercy in how he fucks me. It's fast and hard, long and deep; each time a calculated, purposeful thrust.

"Yes, yes, God yes," I chant, loving the deep pressure.

Our eyes meet as he moves and I'm taken aback to see a little bit of Nate in him. I don't know why or what it is, but it's there. I shouldn't be thinking of him right now and I know that, but for a brief moment, there he was in front of me. Shaking my head to break the connection, I kiss Bain, plunging my tongue into his mouth. He meets mine and we tangle them together, the same way our tangled bodies collide.

Endorphins wash over me and again...I let go. The instant I come, he's right there with me. It's one of the best I've had, so strong and satisfying. I've never had the craving within me calmed, but Bain just did it. When our bodies come back down to earth, Bain asks me, "Do you have any idea how gorgeous you are when you come?"

"Only then?" I ask with my eyebrows scrunched together.

"No, not only then, especially then. God, I want to fuck you over and over again."

"Maybe I'll let you."

You can't stay the night, you can't stay the night, you can't stay the night. Those are the words that I repeat in my head as I lay in Bain's arms. After the pool, we managed to get into the shower, which just turned to more sex. Then, we spent the rest of the day lounging.

"Does staying the night together count if we don't sleep?" Bain asks in between yawns.

I can't hold back the laugh, "Uhhhh, it does because you're exhausted. Get some rest, I'll be back tomorrow."

"How early?" he questions.

"I don't know, when I wake up. Why?"

"Because I want your pussy to be the first thing I feel when I open my eyes."

"I think I can make that happen."

He yawns again and pulls me on top of him. "Sorry, I'm so tired, my dad and I had a long drive back from Virginia today."

"Is that where your mom is?"

"Yeah," he responds, moving a stand of hair out of my face and behind my ear.

"I'm assuming losing your sister is what pushed her over the edge?"

He nods his head and I don't want to pry any further into his family business.

"What about your family, are you close with them?"

he asks.

"I don't have many memories of my parents; they both passed in a car accident when I was a kid."

"Damn, I'm sorry."

"It's all right. I'm lucky to be alive. I was with them when their car was hit by a drunk driver."

"Arion, that's horrible. How old were you?"

"I was four."

"Who raised you after that?"

"My grandma for a little while, but she passed when I was eleven. After that I was bounced around with family and never really had a place to call home.

"I really don't know how you keep plugging along like you do."

"What choice do I have?" I look him in the eyes and rest my hand on his hair. "All of that is the reason I am the way I am. It seems everyone I love, I lose. For me, this is how I protect myself."

"It makes sense, but I guess I just can't really relate. I've never lost anyone besides my sister and the mental blow that took on me was on a whole different level. I mean, she left the world by her own doing. I guess if I'd been through some of the things that you have, then I would feel the same as you and protect myself."

"So I'm not crazy after all?"

"No, you're not. You've been through so much and I admire your strength. I can't say you don't confuse me, but I'll take that mixed with everything else if it means I can do this," he says kissing my lips.

I exhale then respond as we pull away. "I don't want to confuse you, Bain. That's the last thing I want to do."

"I know. I guess I shouldn't be. You've made your rules clear."

"Thank you. Listen, it's getting late. I'm gonna go, but I'll be back."

"And I'll be waiting for you to fulfill that promise."

I smack his chest and he places his hand in the spot I just hit, pretending that I just hurt him.

CHAPTER 16

-Bain-

"Yes, Mom, if you really want me to, I will."

"Thank you, dear."

"Of course. Take care of yourself."

"You too. I love you, Bain."

"Love you too," I tell her and hang up. I'm not sure if Arion heard any of my conversation, but my mom only gets to call once a week and I promised her I'd answer. I know with my dad being away on business, it's unlikely she'll get through to him.

Arion comes into the kitchen, where I'm leaning against the granite countertop and asks, "How is she?"

"She sounds good. It's strange to hear her voice so clear."

"She's sober, it'll change a person."

"It certainly will," I respond.

"Well, she's lucky to have you as her son," she says running her index finger down the middle of my chest. Her touch, and that expression, have my dick tingling.

Arion didn't get here too long ago. It was just as I finally fell into a deep sleep. Last night was hard for me – I thought a lot about Kinsey, my mind was racing about what she went through and I couldn't put it to rest.

She leans in and kisses behind my ear, my breathing calms at the contact of her soft lips. Then my stomach rumbles and she pulls away, staring at me with a smirk on her face.

"Food, then sex?" she asks.

"Works for me, what do you want me to cook?"

"I'll cook, you watch."

I'm happy to oblige and watch her search through the kitchen. Sitting back, she bends over looking in the fridge, pulling out item after item. Her ass is perfect, so plump in her tight pants. It's what caused me to lose it at her work that day when I ran into her.

"What are you making?" I ask.

"It's a surprise."

"Mmh, okay. Do you have to work today?"

"Nope, I'm off 'til Monday.

"Do you want to do something today?"

"Yeah, cook you breakfast, then fuck you."

I can't stop myself from laughing out loud. "After that."

"Bain," she says my name a bit annoyed.

I know where this is going.

"Don't even say anything about your rules, Arion. I know where we stand. Let's get out for a bit. There's supposed to be a nasty storm rolling through in the next few days. Let's get out and enjoy it before then."

"I'll think about it," she says cracking an egg on the side of a glass bowl, then warms up a pan on the stove.

Her resistance to me now makes me wonder how we can fuck the way we do, then she can be so cold at the same time and act like she doesn't even want to hang out together. If she really doesn't want any feelings, why isn't it just sex and then she leaves? I mean, she's the one who came back so early today when I fucked her good yesterday, so I know there's something else there. I decide to change the subject; it'll be easier than pushing her buttons, plus I'm exhausted and on edge.

My phone rings while I watch Arion cook, it's my dad calling. I decline the call, he'll leave a message; he always does. "You can get that," Arion says.

"Nah, it's just my dad."

She's extremely talented in the kitchen, so much more than I am. It doesn't take but a few minutes 'til she sets two heaping plates of French toast on the bar, one for each of us. Jesus, I love her appetite.

After we finish breakfast, I clear our plates and she cleans up the island. Looking over at her body pressed against the granite of the countertop, I lose it. I pin her against it, pressing my already hard cock into her backside.

She turns in my hold and I claim her mouth, pulling her pants down in the process. She does the same to me, removing my shorts, gripping my cock as we kiss. Our mouths tangle and I can't wait to fuck her.

Lifting her up, I don't waste any time sinking inside of her. The walls of her pussy are heaven. She throws her head back bracing her weight on the countertop. I love the sight of her uncovered breasts, taking them in my hands, squeezing the hard mounds, watching confidence beam out of her as we fuck. She's perfect.

My cock pulsates. I'm so hard inside of her, loving how eager she is as she helps me, working her hips against mine.

"Harder, Bain," she murmurs, in between soft noises. I give her what she wants and move her legs at the same time running them up my chest so they rest on either side of my head.

"You want it harder?" I ask, stopping completely with my cock buried all the way inside of her.

"Yes," she shouts. Before I move, I open one of the drawers and pull out the first thing my hand touches – a wooden spoon.

Listening right away, I pick up speed, allowing her cunt to take me out of this world and simultaneously smack the side of one of her ass cheeks with the spoon.

"Fuckkkkkk, yes," she shouts and I hit her again, then move to the other side and then her breasts. I've never done anything like this, but the way it turns her on makes me extremely excited.

"You like this, don't you?" I question breathlessly.

"Mmmmhhhhh," she moans.

Taking a fistful of her hair, I control her and take us both away from the pain and the agony that is reality. With my cock moving in and out of her, it feels so right. All that's left in the pain's place is pleasure; it surges to the tip of my dick.

In this moment while inside Arion, I find the pleasure I've been searching for with pills. A high that will mask all of my pain. And she has given that to me. I don't know how, but she's so unexpectedly and so quickly has become a drug to me. Although the pleasure we share can't last forever, I'll take it any way I can get it right now. I know with her fears, she'll end things sooner rather than later, so I indulge while I can.

With my hands secured tightly around her hips, I fuck her fiercely, giving her all of my ten inches. She doesn't complain, she just takes me, moaning, "Fuck me, Bain." Over and over.

Finally, I have to slow; I can't keep going at this speed. She's about to make me lose it as she clenches her cunt around me and I'm not ready. With slow movements, I spread her pussy, watching my cock move in and out of her.

"Christ, you're beautiful," I murmur.

She doesn't respond with words. However, she does with cries of passion, throwing her head back as she lets her orgasm take over. These actions push me right there with her and we come together. I grunt like an animal as I pump myself bit by bit inside of her. Slowly, I ease my way out of her amazing cunt and she sits up off the granite countertop. I look down at her as she kneels in front of me, then swirls her tongue over the head of my cock. Watching her lick off both of our arousals is such a fucking turn on.

After we dress, I convince her to leave the house with me. I have some shit to do for my mom and I don't want to do it alone. Arion can sense that and I'm grateful. Regardless of the sex, I'm lucky to have her as a friend. It helps to have her next to me in the car. I enjoy her company and how she keeps my mind off of all the bad shit in this world.

"Are you sure you're okay with me doing this with you?" she asks hesitantly. I nod my head and feel bad that this is the first time we get to venture out during the day, and we have to do something like this.

Reaching over, I rest my hand on her thigh. Her generosity is really too much. She didn't need to come; in fact, I don't even know why she did with her fears and all, then she asks if I'm okay with it. Deep down, I'm thankful, I don't know if I could do this alone. My mom asked me to take pictures of the house and the area where Kinsey chose to take her life. I myself have mixed feelings about doing it, but my mom, on the other hand, believes it will help her recovery and the counselors at the rehab center also agree. So if this will help her, then I'll do it, even if I'm uncertain.

"How are you feeling about doing this?" she asks.

"I really just wanna get it done with."

"If it's easier, I can take the pictures for you," she offers reaching down and intertwining our hands.

Glancing down for a brief moment, I stare at our hands, the gesture catching me off guard. "It's okay, we'll do it together," I respond and squeeze her fingers.

For the rest of the ride, we sit in silence. Our hands rest comfortably on my lap and I thank God Arion came with me. Anxiety fills my body, thinking about what we're about to do. Finally we pull up to the house. It looks just like I remember and is still for sale. I've been here once, and it took everything I had, just to drive by, so I know getting out and walking around is going to be hard. Looking at the house as I put the car in park, I try to make sense of why it happened here. I'm baffled.

"Is this it?" she asks.

"Uh-huh."

"Why did she come here?"

"I wonder the same thing every day. Other than the fact that it's vacant, I have no idea."

"Jesus, Bain, I can't imagine what she must've gone through in her mind."

"Me neither." Her words give me a flash of Kinsey and I envision her pulling into the garage after breaking into the house. Using the new garden hose she'd just purchased and…I can't go there.

"Ready?" she asks.

"I guess." She opens her door and I take a deep breath

then do the same. I flip the hood up on my hoodie and hop out of the car. Arion is at my side before I can look and see where she is.

"Wanna take one from here of the front of the house?" she asks.

I take out my cell phone and snap the picture, getting the full view of the entire house. *Just move fast.* It's tall and modern with dark wood wrapped around it. We proceed to walk around. The garage is opposite us and I don't think I can bring myself to go all the way around or to take any pictures of it.

I continue snapping pictures as quick as I can, neither of us saying a word, just completing the task that we came here to do. We make fast work of the job and suddenly without warning we move around to the garage – I freeze. "What?" she asks.

"I...I don't think..."

"It's fine, I understand. Do you want me to finish?" she asks.

"Sure, just take whatever else you think, I'll be in the car." I respond, walking away with my head hung low. I feel bad for leaving her, but my breathing is heavy and in that moment, my world spirals out of control. I know I've seen it before, but for some reason, today, standing in front of that garage, it hits me hard. This is where she killed herself. That is the place where she took her last breath. Once I'm sitting in my car, I rest my head back and close my eyes.

Small breaths are a struggle, but I push them out. I have to. I do my best to stay calm. I don't want to freak out in front of Arion. In that moment, the only thing I know to do is to pop a few pills, but I don't want to in front of her, so I seize the opportunity while I'm alone, opening my console and grabbing a few Xanax, relishing in the flavor on my tongue.

Arion gets in and gives me a slight smile, then holds my hand. I can't sit here in front of this house for another second.

CHAPTER 17

-Kinsey-

"Jesus, I can't wait for you to be home," I tell Bain as I leave school and drive back to the house.

"I know. I miss being there, too. Especially mom's cooking and just being able to relax."

"You don't get a lot of that anymore, do you?"

"Are you kidding me? I'm about to join the NBA, Kins; things here are insane. Every game is flooded with NBA scouts and reporters. Our coach pushes us to play every game like it's our last."

"Well, I know all the hard work is going to pay off. I can't wait to see you get drafted and to come to all your games. You know I'm going to be your number one fan."

"I know and I'm grateful for your support. Listen, I don't have long before practice, but I wanted to call you after I got your text. What's up?"

"Well, I wanted to get Mom a really nice gift, but I'm confused about what she'd like. I mean, what do you buy the woman who has everything?"

"Did you ask Dad?"

I can't help but laugh. "Yeah, he said 'ask your brother.'"

"Of course he did. What about a weekend getaway for the two of them, like to Napa or something?"

"That's a great idea! Mom's always saying how she misses California. Maybe she could visit Aunt Patti when she's there, too?" I tell Bain.

"It sounds like a great idea to me. Why don't you look into booking it and let me know if you want to bounce any more ideas around? I gotta run though, we have practice."

I hang up with my brother, just before telling him about my date with Anthony tonight. I don't know what I was thinking. Bain's so protective over me; he would never understand why I am going out with a teacher. Pulling up to the house, my dad is in the garage.

I head towards him rather than going inside. "Hey, kid," he says, with a smile from ear to ear.

"Hey, Dad. What are you doing?"

"Just cleaning out the car before I head out of town."

"Where are you going?"

"Philly."

"Nice, at least you can drive."

"That's the truth."

"Where's mom?"

"She went to have drinks with some of the girls."

"Oh good. So I just talked to Bain about what to get her and he gave me the best idea ever. You still have her birthday week off of work right?"

"Yeah, why?"

"I can't tell you, silly. This is for both of you guys."

"Kinsey, you know I hate surprises," he says in a firm tone.

"As do I and you always make me deal with them." I walk off with my dad begging for more details, but I ignore him.

CHAPTER 18

-Arion-

"So you're dating him," Aubrey accuses me.

"Hell no. Why would you even say that?"

"I don't know, maybe because you haven't been home much this past week."

I glare at her. "Aubrey, I was gone for the weekend. That's far from a week. We've just chilled together."

"Well, it sure as hell feels like there's more going on here."

I get off the couch to refill my water bottle, honestly wanting to ignore her. "You can deny all you want, but let me ask you this. Why's this guy so different? I haven't seen you act like this since Nate."

"He's no different than Brady or anyone else. But he's been through some really fucked up shit, so I've been trying to be there for him, and in the process he's turned out to be a really good friend."

"You just met him."

"What's that matter?"

"Is he your friend or do you fuck?"

"Seriously, Aubrey, what's your fucking problem? Yeah, we fuck, you know that's how I am. He's also a friend. Is that a bad thing?"

She shakes her head, "No, it's not, I'm just worried about you and trying to figure out why he's got your head so twisted."

"Dude, I appreciate your concern, but…" I trail off and decide to head out for a run rather than start an argument with her. She's only trying to understand things. Plus, I feel Nate pulling me to our spot. Maybe if I go there, I'll get some answers on how to handle all of this. I know arguing with Aubrey isn't going to help anything.

I appreciate her concern, I really do, but I need to figure out what's inside my own head, myself.

"I'm gonna go for a run. Can we talk later?"

"Of course. I don't want you to be mad at me. I just care about you."

"I know and I appreciate that. I'll be back soon." I give her a hug, then head into my room, putting on a tight pair of black leggings, a hoodie, and my running shoes. Aubrey's not in the living room when I leave, so I grab my cell phone and bolt. The air is crisp and the sky is gray. It looks like we might get some rain today. I know running in this weather will burn my lungs, but it'll also take the pain away. We live just a few blocks from the beach and within a few minutes, the pavement beneath my feet changes to sand. I make my way down towards the water, the familiar sound soothing me. The waves are light, but still crash against the shore. My legs pick up speed, taking me on the long journey to my final destination – my spot with Nate. The place where he asked me to marry him, we never had that dream come true as he was deployed quicker than we expected.

For some reason, it's hard to clear my mind today. Normally a good run is just what I need, but instead, all I hear are Bain and Aubrey's voices swirling in my head. *So you're dating him? Christ, you're beautiful.*

I don't even know how to comprehend these two statements. They have my mind on a tilt and spinning in a way I've never experienced. Then automatically, all my stress washes away the moment my phone rings and I see it's Bain calling. For some reason, he has that effect on me. I inhale deeply, trying to calm my breathing, but it's useless. Breathlessly, I answer, "Hey you."

"Hey to you. How are you?"

"I'm all right."

"What's wrong? You sound out of breath."

"I'm out on a run."

"Arion, are you kidding me?"

"What?" I ask confused.

"There's a goddamn storm on the way."

I realize then that it's starting to get nasty outside. The wind around me howls and there are no other people out. "It's not that bad," I respond, looking into the gray sky.

"The fuck it's not. Where are you? I'm coming to get

you."

"No, Bain, it's fine, I can run back home."

"Where the FUCK are you?" he yells. "Goddammit, Arion!"

"Ashbury Park," I quickly respond, not liking his tone.

"Fuck, that's far from your house."

"No, it's not, Bain. I don't know why you're freaking out, it's not even raining."

"Because it's going to be pouring frozen rain soon and it's windy as fuck. Where exactly are you? It won't take me long."

I explain to him where I am and within minutes, he arrives. Before I can open the passenger door, he leans over and opens it for me. He looks hot as fuck, dressed in a black t-shirt, his arms bulging through the material. He's wearing dark jeans and has a soft beanie covering his hair.

"Are you all right?"

I nod my head and buckle my seatbelt. "Thank you for coming to get me."

He turns the heat up and says, "Of course. I was in the area, so it's no big deal."

I can't help, but smirk at him. "What were you doing in this area?"

He shakes his head and I don't push the question, because inside, I'm happy that he's here. It was starting to get cold outside and really windy, even if I want to act like it wasn't. It's just starting to rain outside, so if I would have made it to Nate's and my spot, then I would have been drenched. Plus, the cold and wet run home would have been no fun.

"Where are we going?" I ask.

"My house. Is that okay?"

"Yeah." His place is perfect and I know he can clear my mind.

Bain doesn't say much on the drive and neither do I. He knows our arrangement and clearly we are both in need of the distraction. But in the pit of my stomach, I feel like we are pushing those limits. Yes, we know the rules. Which in all honesty, when I'm around Bain, I wish I didn't have, but sadly…I do. My past fucked me. With the rules, he should have picked me up solely to fuck, but I can sense there's more going on with him. He's keeping something from me and that's why he was close to my house.

We pull up to his home and he parks in the garage. Then we head inside and the warmth engulfs me. I almost shiver with how good it feels to have my entire body warmed.

"Are you still cold?" he asks, wrapping his arms around me.

Looking into his eyes, there is genuine concern etched across his face. "I'm better now, thank you."

"Good. Will you please not run again when it's that crazy out?"

I nod my head and follow Bain's lead as he walks us to the couch. We sit facing each other. He places his face in his hands and I know right then that something is truly bothering him.

"What's the matter?" I ask.

"They found new evidence in Kinsey's case."

"Evidence?"

"Yeah."

"What does that even mean?" I ask bewildered.

"There was a fingerprint in her car that hasn't matched anyone."

"Why are you just finding out about this now?"

"I don't know. But I've had a bad feeling about the investigator from the beginning and my dad was recently contacted by the FBI. Apparently, he knew about it all along and when it didn't come back with a match, he let it go."

"The FBI, why are they involved?"

"You know, I'm not sure. But I'm thankful."

"Does this mean she didn't...?" I trail off, not sure if I should speak the words out loud or not.

"It means that someone else was driving her car that day. It was found on the turn signal."

"Jesus, are you serious?"

"That's what they told my dad."

"I can't imagine what's going through your mind."

"Honestly, I just want to forget about it right now. I held onto hope for weeks after she went missing, thinking she was still alive. That's why I needed to see you. I'm sorry if I acted like a dick."

"It's fine. You're going through hell. If I'm your distraction, then I'm happy to be," I respond, scooting over and straddling his lap.

Taking both of my hands, I wrap them into the back of his hair and pull his mouth to mine. I watch as his eyes close and he exhales heavily. With his mouth slacked open, I lean in, moaning, and kiss him. Giving him all of me. Wanting to take away every bit of pain that he's feeling. For me, he does that every time we're together.

He takes his hands and slides them underneath the back of my hoodie. His warm fingers press into my skin before he pulls away and rips it above my head. Then I remove my bra and watch how his eyes look at my breasts, before he squeezes one and takes the other into his mouth. I push into him, loving the feeling of his lips, and grind my hips against his erection as it strains his pants.

Reaching down, he unzips them. I scoot back and kneel next to him as he strokes himself. Then I take all of him in my mouth. He tastes delicious; his dick is already so hard. Moving my mouth up and down on his swollen member, makes my pussy yearn for pleasure. He reaches for me, rubbing me hard through my clothing. Pulling away, I finally stop and we both undress all the way. I help him with his shirt, lifting it over his head, and then push him down onto the couch.

"I can't wait to be inside your cunt," he says, as I straddle him and guide his cock inside of me. As soon as he is in all the way, I lean back, bracing my hands on his thighs and begin to move, raising and lowering my hips. Bain holds my hips and bucks underneath me. With his head leaned against the couch, he has his lip tucked into his teeth and eyes tightly shut.

I keep my movements steady and don't have a filter on my noises. Bain fills me, giving me the pleasure I've been craving. "Fuck," I cry loudly, tightening my pussy around him. His size still catches me off guard. Tilting my head, I concentrate on the greatness that is two bodies becoming one. Our skin slaps together, as his dick rubs me vigorously. My body begins to combust with pleasure and with urgency, I slam hard up and down, letting my release take over. I wait for Bain to do the same, but his noises never come. He seems to be even and calm, which is not like him – at all. Running my fingers through his hair, I ask, "Is everything okay?"

"Yeah, why?"

"You just…You didn't come."

"Yeah, I did, right in the beginning. I don't know what you're doing to me or my cock, but I like it."

CHAPTER 19

-Bain-

Staring at Arion asleep in my bed, I almost feel guilty for not waking her. I check the clock and it's 12:47am. I should take her home; I know how she feels about staying the night. But the truth is…I don't want to, she makes everything so much better. Being around her makes all my worries so minuscule.

Especially considering the morning we had, she really turned things around and made me forget about all of the bad shit. She also did a damn good job at keeping my mind busy. It was nice to talk to her about a lot of the thoughts swirling around my head. It makes me feel not so crazy getting them off my chest and having someone that agrees with me. Someone that's experienced a loss a lot like I have.

I know losing Kinsey isn't the same as losing the love of your life. However, her loss impacted me to the point where I spiraled and lost touch with the person I once was. I'm addicted to pills, my mom is in rehab, and my family is basically torn. We're not the same people we used to be.

Arion rolls over, curling into a little ball. I leave a kiss on her cheek and get up to get dressed. I know I have to take her home. I owe her that much. I respect her wishes and won't ruin that trust. Once I'm dressed, I lean over her, brushing her soft, blonde hair out of her face, and kiss her lips. "Wake up, sleepyhead. We gotta get going."

She doesn't respond to me. I know she's tired. "Come on, A. We gotta go, babe." The word 'babe' leaves my mouth before I know what I've said. *Jesus, what's wrong with me? No feelings!*

Again she doesn't respond and I nudge her a little. "Come on."

"No," she grumbles.

"No, let's go," I say tickling her back with the tips of my fingers.

"Nuh-uh, I'm fine," she responds and rolls into a tighter ball.

"You sure?" I ask.

She nods her head and I leave the bedroom. I mean, what can I do? If she says she's fine, then she's fine. I know what I want to do is strip down stark naked and cuddle her, but I can't. I think I'm having these kinds of feelings because she told me not to. So instead, I make my way to the couch.

I know having her in my house for the night will make it almost impossible for me to sleep, so I pray for some darkness. Before I hit the couch, I check that everything is locked and look in at her one last time. She's so small and comfortable in my bed. She's naked from the sex we had earlier, and that hair...I've always been a sucker for blondes.

Going back to the living room, I turn the light off and plop down on the couch. Turning the TV on, I remember there isn't shit on as it's one in the morning. I roll over, covering myself with the throw from the back. The moment I close my eyes, I'm haunted with images of Kinsey and someone hurting her. I open them and stare at the ceiling. *Dammit, I'm fucked up.* The fingerprint doesn't mean shit. I'm sure it was from one of her friends driving her car.

I remind myself to think of Arion – she's my distraction.

Waking up, my hand is clutched tightly around my cock. God, it feels good. As I jerk myself, I imagine the inside of Arion's pussy, so warm and tight. I have a tight grip around the base and suddenly realize she's here. *What the fuck am I doing?*

I pull my hand away and roll to my side, glancing around the room. The clock on the wall reads 11:18am. Sitting up, I stare at my erection, mentally pleading with it to go down. Once it does, I make my way to my bedroom, but Arion isn't there. Nervously, I glance around. She can't be far since she doesn't have a car. She's probably swimming, but the pool is empty and calm. Frantically, I begin to check each room.

She's not here. Fuck, she left.

Walking back to the couch, I grab my cell phone. She hasn't sent me a text or called. I dial her number and it rings a few times then goes to voicemail. I call her again and can't believe that she really left without saying goodbye or anything.

Goddammit, I knew I should have taken her home last night. I bet anything when she woke up, she was freaked out, or pissed off for staying the night. I shoot her a text. I need to know that she's okay.

Did you make it home all right? That's all I send, I don't want to sound like a lunatic, but I'm also worried about where she is.

Staring at my screen, I begin to panic, hoping she's safe. I start a pot of coffee to distract myself, then pop a few pills before getting in the shower. *Busy, busy, busy, keep your mind busy!* I repeat the words in my head as I step out of the shower and start to dry myself off. Then my phone rings and I answer it right away. "Arion?"

"Uhh, no. This is Lieutenant Baker with the FBI, is this Bain Adams?"

Fuck!

"Uh-huh." I grumble, instantly regretting answering the phone.

"Mr. Adams, do you have a moment?"

"Yeah." My tone is somber, what else am I supposed to say? I want to slam the phone down and say fuck off because nothing is going to bring Kinsey back.

"I was hoping we could talk about that print we found in your sister's car."

"Does it have to be today? I'm kinda busy." I lie.

"I'm sorry to ask, but yes, if there's any way you could, I would be grateful."

"Sure," I grumble.

"Thank you. Also, could you and your family please not have any contact with Detective Eldridge? I'll fill you in on the details once you get here."

I agree and hang up, kind of in shock. *What the hell happened?* Suddenly I feel like I'm about to hyperventilate. Instinctively, I dial Arion's number, but she doesn't answer, so I call my dad.

"Bain, is everything all right?"

"Fuck, Dad, I don't know." My tone is laced with panic.

"Goddammit, Bain, what's going on?"

Leaning my forearm against the wall, I stand there with my head resting on it, searching for the words.

"Son, my flight is about to take off so I have to turn my phone off. Please talk to me, tell me that you're all right."

Exhaling loudly I stay strong for my dad. Taking a few deep breaths before I respond. "I'm fine, I just got a call from the FBI."

"Why are they calling you?"

"They need to talk to me about the print found in Kinsey's car."

"You don't need to go. Not if it's gonna upset you like this."

"I'm fine, really I am. I…I just had a moment and got upset."

"Are you sure?"

"Yeah, he also said for us to not have any contact with Eldridge."

"Sir, you need to turn your phone off," I hear a woman in the background say.

"Why did he say that?"

"I don't know, I'll call you after I meet with him, though."

"Stay strong, son. Are you sure you're all right?"

"I'm good. Fly safely."

"I will. I'll call you as soon as I land."

We hang up and although I told my dad that I was okay, I feel weak and sick to my stomach. *Pull your shit together, Bain.* I do my best to snap out of it. This isn't how Kinsey would want me to be. She would expect me to hold my head high and be strong for her. I should be happy that the FBI is finally involved and *has* made progress.

Heading out of the house, I program the address into my GPS. It's in the city and with traffic, it takes me close to an hour to arrive, but finally I do.

The building is tall, sleek, and black. I put my car in park and contemplate taking a few pills to calm my nerves. Screw it; I've got nothing to lose at this point. Walking inside, I say a silent prayer, hoping that I can keep my shit together. Emotions swirl around me as I head to meet with the man that might finally give me some answers.

CHAPTER 20

-Kinsey-

I really wish I had Anthony's phone number. I'm a nervous wreck waiting for him, and I feel like I'm not even at the right place. Checking the clock on my cell phone, it's 6:04pm. Okay, maybe I'm overreacting a tad. I am early.

Standing up, I head outside going into the cool evening. Pulling my coat a little tighter around me, I look at all the people as they bustle by and then…there he is. I catch sight of him right away, from far off in the distance.

It takes him a moment to see me. He walks with such confidence and his eyes light up the moment he sees me from across the square. He looks relaxed as he approaches. "Hey, sorry, I missed my train," he says wrapping me in a warm, more than friendly hug.

I squeeze back, not expecting the gesture, but liking it. He pulls away and very chastely kisses my cheek. "You look beautiful tonight."

"Thank you," I respond with a stomach full of butterflies.

"Did you check in yet?"

"Yeah, but the wait is super long."

"Let's grab something to go and eat at my place."

"Are you sure?" I ask, a little nervous to be alone with him.

"As long as you don't mind driving, yes."

"I don't mind at all."

"Let's go," he says and grabs my hand, waiting for me to lead him in the direction of my car. Dammit, brain, work. Once I get my feet and head to cooperate, we walk, and he lifts our hands kissing my knuckles.

"Thank you for coming out with me."

I just smile; I mean what am I supposed to say? The guy takes my breath away, making speaking around him pretty difficult.

CHAPTER 21

-*Arion*-

For the fourteenth time today, my thumb hovers over the send button as I reread my text to Bain. Again, I decide on deleting it and go back to hovering over the call button. I swear I've been doing this for close to an hour, which is completely absurd.

Tilting my head back against the wrought iron of my headboard, I stare up at the ceiling. It's Bain, he'll understand. *Fuck, no, he won't.* He'll want more, he'll end up hurting me and leaving me like my Nate did.

I slam the phone down on my bed and slink back under the covers, where I've been all day. Yeah, call me pathetic. I don't really give a fuck. My mind is fucking me worse than any words you could ever say.

There's a knock on my door, then I see Aubrey's head poke in. "Hey, you don't hate me, do you?"

"Of course I don't."

"Good, I'm sorry if I pissed you off yesterday. I was just being protective."

"It's fine, you've always been protective over me. I shouldn't expect that to change now."

"You're right, I have and I always will. So if you really like this guy, let me meet him."

Rolling over, I squint my eyes at her. Is she serious? But there is genuine concern in her tone.

"I'll think about it."

"You'll think about it," she repeats.

I nod my head. I can't really promise her that she can meet Bain. Not after I snuck out of his house this morning and took a cab home like a psycho.

Will you just let me know that you're all right?

Christ, he's so sweet. I can't ignore him any longer and text back. **I'm good. Sorry about this morning.**

You home?

Yeah.

He doesn't respond and ten minutes later I hear a knock on the front door. Instantly, I know it's him. I rush around my room, trying to figure out what to do with myself. Then I hear Aubrey answer and I don't waste another minute. The second I come into his view, they both stop speaking and he charges towards me. Placing both hands on either side of my face he says, "You said you were all right."

"I am," I respond leaning into his touch.

"No, you're not. I can see it in your eyes and you're

wearing the same clothes as yesterday."

Out of the corner of my eye, I catch Aubrey slink into her room. Blinking at Bain a few times, I'm not sure how to answer him.

"I'm fine," I finally say.

"Don't lie to me. You left this morning and I haven't been able to get a hold of you all day. I can see it."

Turning my back on him, I head into my bedroom and clamber onto my bed. He's right behind me, not allowing me to turn my back on him, as I try to bury myself into my pillow. "I'm not leaving 'til you tell me what's going on."

"I...I'm sorry I stayed the night last night."

"Are you? Because I'm not, the only thing I'm sorry for is that I didn't sleep with you in my arms. It didn't matter that I slept on the couch, because you still left."

Rolling over, I face him and can tell that he's dead serious. However, inside I feel like I'm betraying Nate by giving into my feelings for Bain.

He holds me tight, letting out a big sigh. I can't believe my actions affected him like they did. In that moment, I feel horrible for acting how I did. Nate is gone and Bain...Bain is right here with me and all I've been worrying about is myself, not caring what I was doing to him.

"You're right. I'm not sorry. I'm just scared."

"Don't be scared. It's just me, A. Nothing needs to change with us, except you trusting me a little more. You don't need to run from me, you can run to me. Let your walls down, Arion. I promise I won't break them."

Tears fill my eyes at the thought of putting myself out there. I know if I do it again and with anyone, I want it to be Bain...but can I?

"Can we just act like all of this never happened?"

He smirks at me and kisses the side of my mouth, still holding me tightly against him. "Are you going to let me in?" I nod my head biting my bottom lip. "Then if that's what you need, yes. Just trust me, okay?"

"Okay," I whisper, now lying completely underneath of him. "Wanna tell me what's going on with you?" I ask, knowing him well enough to see the pain in his eyes.

He exhales loudly, resting his head on my chest and holds me tighter than ever. "Come on, Bain, if you want me to let you in, then you have to do the same."

"I met with the FBI today."

"About your sister?"

"Uh-huh."

"What did they say?"

"They don't think she killed herself.

"Oh my God, are you fucking serious? Why?"

"That print they found in her car has gone missing. Someone hacked into the computer system and deleted it. They are unable to find the hard copy, as well."

"Fuck, Bain, how does that happen?"

"That piece of shit detective did it, I know it. Now he's under investigation because there have been so many red flags since the FBI took over."

"Jesus, I'm sorry. I'm so sorry that I wasn't there to go through this with you."

"It's okay, my mind has been a mess today, but you're here now. I just don't know what to think – what to believe anymore. For so long I was convinced that she didn't do this – that she wouldn't. I didn't have a choice, but to believe that she *did*, so I came to terms with it, in a way. I mean what other choice did I have? Now, it's like I've been kicked in the gut and I'm back at square one."

"I don't think you can get ahead of yourself yet. Just live in this moment, right here, right now.

"But Arion, someone could've killed her and still be out there. That absolutely fucking infuriates me."

I really don't know what to say or how to make any of this better, so I do what I told him I would. I open up and try to relate. "When I lost Nate, I went through a long period of denial, as well. It was like my mind kept saying no way, no way, no way is he really gone. Especially because he was MIA and that gave me hope. But eventually, they recovered parts of his body. It's not the same as Kinsey's death, but they have their similarities. Then when the news came that they had found him…" I get choked up going back to that day. I can remember right where I was sitting, at his parents' house when the knock on the door came. I can picture Barb as she fell to her knees and how Jeff just held her. Bain rubs my back. Jesus, I haven't talked about these events to anyone. So I proceed because this needs to be done and I told him I'd let him in. "I knew no matter how much it hurt to hear the news, he was gone and gone for real. I had to face it. I know it's not exactly the same as how Kinsey passed, but in a way…it is. Both of them are gone, plain and simple." Tears stream out the sides of my eyes as I speak. "I know nothing will ever bring them back to us. We might be stuck here and in pain, but they can never be hurt again. And one thing you can take from all of this, is knowing that she didn't make the decision to take her own life. The FBI will find who did this, that's what they are trained to do."

Both of us lie in silence, neither saying a word. The contentment of listening to each other breathing is so soothing. It's been a long time since I've felt this calm – this safe – and this at ease.

My shirt is moist from his tears and his breathing. I hope my words helped to ease a bit of the pain that Bain is experiencing. In the short period of time I've known him, I know he's someone special and someone that's supposed to be in my life, whatever the reason may be.

Jeff called and said Zeus hasn't been feeling well. My stomach is in knots from the fear that something is wrong with my baby boy. Parking in front of the familiar house, I hop out and head in, noticing that Zeus isn't greeting me at the door or the windows.

I see Jeff inside and he waves me in. "Hi there, kiddo," he says wrapping me in a side hug.

"Hey, where is he? Is he okay?"

"He's all right. He's out back."

We both walk to the back door where Zeus is moping around the backyard, with his tail bent down and ears back. I open the screen and whistle, calling him over to me. His ears perk right up and he runs to me.

"Hey, buddy, how are you?" I ask scratching behind his ears.

He leans into my touch and I bring him inside.

I take my usual seat on the floor. "Go get your ball," I tell Zeus. He walks off and comes back with it gingerly hanging from his mouth. Then curls up next to me and I ask Jeff. "How long has he been like this?"

"Just a few days."

"Has he been eating normally?"

"Yeah, everything seems to be normal, just the fact that he's a little sluggish."

"Do you think he got into anything?"

Jeff tilts his head thinking about my question. "No, I don't think so."

"Do you think I should make a vet appointment?"

"I honestly don't know if there is much that they could do. He seems normal aside from his attitude."

I exhale loudly and remember when Nate and I got this little guy. Well, he's not so little any more, but to me he'll always be that small, playful pup we picked out when we graduated. "You'll feel better, bud, just give it some time," I tell him.

"How have you been?" Jeff asks me.

"All right, thanks for asking."

"You look good, happier."

"I am. I've been focusing on taking each day as it comes. Not having expectations for it or what the outcome will be. Also, I met a friend who's been through a similar situation and we've been good support for one another."

I hope I'm not overstepping any boundaries by telling Jeff about Bain.

"That's good to hear. Did she also lose a significant other?"

"Uhhh…It's actually a he. And he lost his sister, but the situations are kinda the same. He went a few weeks not knowing if she was alive or not, a lot like we did."

He nods slowly, processing the words. I don't want to disappoint or hurt Jeff. That's the last thing that I want to do.

"Arion, I want you to know that Barb and I view you as a daughter, so your happiness is very important to us. Maybe one day down the road, we could meet the guy who brings this smile to your face."

I smile getting off the floor and hug him. "Thank you. That really means a lot to me. His name is Bain, I think you would like him."

"I'm sure we would. Listen, I gotta run to an appointment. Are you gonna stay with Zeus for a bit?"

"I wish I could, but I'm gonna go too. If you say he's good minus his attitude, I know he'll perk up. I'll text you later to see how he's doing, okay?"

"Absolutely."

As I pull away from Jeff and Barb's, I feel like I just broke the news to my father that I'm dating someone and he accepts it. I know Jeff is most certainly *not* my father, however, I have always looked up to him in that sense and value his opinion. Checking the clock, I notice there isn't much time before I need to be ready to head to the basketball game with Bain. This should be a good distraction for both of us. I won tickets through my work, which never happens, and surprisingly, he seemed excited. I was worried to ask him at first and thought he would for sure say no.

My phone rings on the drive and I answer it.

"Hey, girl," Aubrey says.

"What's up?" I ask, considering I just saw her, when she stopped by my work today.

"I totally forgot to ask you if wanted to hit the gym with me."

"I totally would, but Bain and I are going to the Knicks game. I can go with you tomorrow night."

"Okay, that sounds good. You guys have fun tonight, I'm gonna run."

"Thanks, you have fun too."

I hang up as I park my car in front of the apartment. I make my way inside, noticing a missed text from Bain. *Can I come over early and fuck you?*

I can't help, but laugh out loud opening my front door. **Do you really need to ask?**

I didn't want to assume. I'm on my way.

You do realize that the game starts at 7:00.

I don't need that long. What kind of animal do you think I am?

Uhhh, the kind that likes to fuck and fuck a lot.

All right, enough with the F word. Get your ass naked and ready for me.

I agree and begin peeling off my Starbucks clothes and get into the steaming hot shower.

The water feels blissful. I'm tempted to stay in here and make Bain come find me when he arrives. But I can't remember if I left the door unlocked or not. So instead, I quickly wash, shave, rinse, and get out. As I cover my body in lotion, I'm startled by the figure standing in my doorway. Staring back at me with that burning look, is Bain.

"Hi," I whisper.

"You need to lock your door," he responds.

"I left it open for you."

"I appreciate that, but your safety is important. Now get over here and let me taste those amazing lips."

CHAPTER 22

-Bain-

Listening to my order, she walks to me stark naked. Her signature Arion smirk is plastered across her face and I can't stop myself from pressing her into the door.

Taking her face in one of my hands, I lean in and kiss her. Jesus, her lips are like heaven. With my free hand I run it down her body, noticing how every bit of her fits so perfectly against my palm. Removing my mouth from hers, I breathe her in and look into her eyes. There's an alluring look that's driving me mad, mixed with her scent — it all intoxicates me. She smells so sweet, yet there's a hint of something I can't pinpoint.

I kiss her again, trailing kisses down her neck and across her chest. A moan escapes her and she catches me off guard when she grabs my dick through my pants. I push myself into her, grinding against her hand like it's her pussy. Pulling away, she fumbles with my pants and I stop her. "I will fuck you and I can't promise that we'll make it to the game."

"It's worth the risk."

I chuckle at her brazenness. I should have guessed that she wouldn't have a problem missing a basketball game in order to fuck. I can't take my eyes off of her as I shrug my pants down, leaving them bunched at my ankles. As she steps towards me, I reach down and touch her perfect little cunt. There's not a spot of hair on her and the moment my fingers move in between her soft folds, my cock aches for her.

"Mhh, you're wet. You want me to fuck you, don't you?"

"God, yes," she says resting her arms around my neck. With that response, I sink inside of her tight cunt, burrowing my cock in as far as I can fit. Our bodies mold so perfectly. Her heart pulsates under my hold, my size almost filling her completely.

I lift her up and she gasps. "Wrap your legs around me," I order. Tonight I'm not holding back. This is who I am when it comes to sex. Lately, the pills have put me at a bit of a disadvantage. But now I'm in my zone, exactly where I need to be. I've dealt with nothing but pain and despair for over half a year. But when I'm with Arion, I don't have to pretend and I let that all go. God, I love this. Pleasure surges through me. Quietly, I pound her as she hangs on to me with passion drenching from her.

The room is silent except for her noises and our skin slapping against each other. "Is your roommate here?" I ask, stopping for only a brief moment to try and drown out some of the noise, because I need to fuck her harder.

"No."

Picking up speed, I show no mercy and slam inside of her. Without Aubrey here, there's no reason to be quiet. Arion doesn't complain, with her back against the wall and not a thread of clothing on. She's in her zone and by far the sexiest thing I've ever seen. I indulge and enjoy having her all alone.

Thinking back, I remember wondering when our last time would be. I'm not the kind of guy who sleeps around; I just don't. I've never started a relationship like this, if that's what you could even call what we are doing – a relationship. Whatever it is, I can say without a doubt that I am one-hundred percent ready to take the next step with this girl, letting her open up to me, and building her trust.

Her body tenses and I can tell that she's about to let go. I keep my eyes on her. Watching the way her neck glistens with sweat, small moans roll out of her as she knots her fingers tightly into my hair.

Our eyes stay connected 'til that moment, 'til pure bliss takes over and reality washes everything away. Her body shakes and trembles in my hold. "Yes, Bain, fuck me, make me come."

Taking my hand, I place it around the back of her neck as her words fade out into louder moans. She lets her legs drop and stands on her own. Without missing a beat, I bring her pleasure to the surface and make her come good and hard. Watching what I can do to her, makes my cock explode. My release is so intense, that pleasure shoots to the back of my head.

But I can't close my eyes; with Arion, I never can. Staring at her panting while I pump myself inside of her is such a goddamn turn on. With a few strands of her blonde locks down and around her face, I brush them away and slow my movements.

"Do you have any idea how fucking hot you are?"

Suddenly, she becomes shy. I'm not sure why, but she turns her head away from me.

"You don't need to flatter me, Bain; you already have me where you want me."

"I'm not trying to flatter you. I'm speaking the truth."

"Well, you're too sweet. So are we going to this game, or are we gonna fuck?"

"I just fucked you," I respond, moving in and out of her. "But I'm down for more."

She looks at me, whimpering a little. I can tell how much she already loves the sensation. "Do you wanna go?" she asks me.

"I wanna do what you wanna do."

"Let's go, we can fuck any time."

I can't help, but laugh out loud. "Coming from the girl who doesn't go on dates herself. I believe I just gave you an out."

"Whatever, Bain, it's not an out. You know you wanna go just as much as I wanna watch all those sweaty men run around. Plus, I've never sat courtside. It should be fun."

"You didn't tell me we were sitting courtside," I respond and finally pull out of her.

"I swear I did."

"Trust me, I would have remembered that."

"Even more of a reason to go, right?"

Suddenly I feel nervous as I dress again and sit back on her bed. Being that close to the game and all, I'm bound to run into someone. "Bain, are you gonna answer me?"

"I'm sorry, I didn't hear you."

"I just said it gives us even more of a reason to go, you know with seats like that."

"Yeah," I say and nod my head.

She looks at me questioningly and then disappears into her closet. I lean back trying to control my breathing, it's erratic – a little out of control. The worst part is I didn't bring any pills with me tonight. I want to stop taking the stupid things. They make me a different person – I *need* to stop. Arion gives me the drive to do it, but in times like this, when I feel nervous, I'm not sure how to handle myself or what's going on. I hate that I've become so dependent on them.

"How does this look?" she asks, standing before me in a pair of tight, white skinny jeans, a loose, flow, gold shirt, and matching heels.

"It looks fucking hot."

"Glad you approve. Let's hit the road."

I swallow hard and tightly hold her hand on the way to

my car. Once we are driving, it gives me something to focus on, but I know she can sense how quiet I am.

"Wanna talk about what's bothering you?" she asks.

I shake my head and instantly feel like a pussy. I've asked her to let me in and open up, but when she asks me…I can't.

"Come on, you're not going to have any fun like this. You're a ball of nerves."

I glance at her briefly; she's sitting facing me as I drive. I can't keep my eyes on her for long though and have to put them back on the road.

"I haven't been keeping this from you, okay? I want you to know that first and foremost. What's bothering me is part of who I used to be before losing Kinsey. You only know the Bain I am now, since losing her."

"You can tell me anything." She reassures me and grabs my hand.

"You know I played college basketball, right?"

"Yeah."

"Well, it's been talked about that I'd be a top ten pick in this year's draft. With us sitting courtside, I feel like I'm more likely to have someone recognize me. Whether it's a scout, or a reporter, or a coach. I mean, who knows? I just don't wanna have to answer the questions of where I've been and why I left school, you know? I mean, people should know, but still, I don't want to get into all that."

She nods her head and twirls a piece of her blonde hair around her finger. "You don't have to tell anybody anything."

"What am I supposed to say?" I question her, a bit surprised that she's not shocked by my news of me possibly being drafted so high into NBA.

"If anyone has the balls to even ask you, which I doubt they will, tell them you've had family matters to attend to and you haven't ruled out the NBA."

I can't help, but laugh out loud. "What's so funny?" she asks.

"I have ruled out the NBA."

"Why the fuck would you do that, Bain?" she snaps.

I look over at her. She's got her eyebrows creased and is dead serious waiting for my response. "I don't have the desire to play anymore."

"Well, get the motherfucking desire. Bain, do you have any idea what you're throwing away? It's a once in a lifetime opportunity. I mean, you are literally one in a million. I didn't know your sister, but I can almost guarantee that she would be livid to know that you are just letting those dreams go. Any family member would agree with me. Please just think hard about it. I know losing her has been horrible, but in five years do you wanna look back and still be living at home with your parents in Jersey, or do you wanna be living your dreams?"

She pulls her hand away from mine and just shakes her head, crossing her arms over her chest.

"I'm sorry," I say.

"Don't be sorry to me, just do something about it.

This is your life and only you're in control of your future."

I let her words soak in getting off the Garden State Parkway. I haven't had an ass chewing like that in months and needed it. She's right, this is *my* life and *I* have control over it. Once we've found a lot close to the stadium, I put the car in park and I turn towards her, but she goes to get out. Grabbing her arm, I stop her and she looks at me.

"Thank you," I say, truly grateful for her. Her words replay through my mind like a broken record. *In five years do you still want to be living at home with your parents, or do you wanna be living you dreams?* I know deep down, I have some soul searching to do. I need to figure out what I'm going to do with my life. But she's right; Kinsey would be pissed at me if she could see me now.

Leaning over, I place my palm against her cheek, cupping her beautiful face. She leans into my touch and I connect our lips, placing mine over hers. She's so warm as I stare at her, molding our mouths together.

"Ready?" I ask.

"Yup."

We both exit the car and bundle up. It's a cold spring night. Arion sparks up a cigarette and I wrap her tightly in my hold. A light drizzle is starting to fall.

"How would reporters know you anyways?"

I chuckle at her question. *This is not going to go well, I can tell already.* "I might regret saying this later, but don't ever Google me."

"Really?"

"Yeah, there are some embarrassing interviews on YouTube from my freshman year in college."

"I so know what I'm doing tonight."

I squeeze her ass. "Don't! I mean it."

We both laugh and I exhale heavily. I'm actually a bit excited to see the game. I've started to miss basketball lately, and because of Arion, I have a plan as to what I'll say if anyone asks where I've been.

CHAPTER 23

-Kinsey-

"So, this is it," Anthony says, pointing to his modern home.

"I love it! Is the ocean on the other side?"

"It is. Let's head in and I'll show you." Getting out of the car I hear the waves crash onto shore. The noise brings back so many memories. Even though I don't live far from the water, I don't visit it enough. Anthony unlocks the wooden front door and gestures me in. At first sight, I can see the vast expansion of water that is the beautiful ocean and I wish I had my camera.

I walk to the back window hearing him shut the door. "Come on, let's go out," he says, setting our food down on the table. I follow his lead and go outside. I have to blink a few times to make sure what I'm seeing is for real. The ocean is not but twenty yards away.

"Do you like the water?" he asks me.

"I love it. When I was younger, we used to spend the summers at my family's beach house in St. John's, but now that my brother and I are grown, we hardly ever go."

"Ahh, you have a brother. Older or younger?"

I smile, looking over at him as his hands are tucked tightly into the pockets of his pants. "We're twins, so there's not much of an age difference. But if you ask him he'd tell you he's older by a minute and a half."

"Do you have a picture?"

"Yeah," I respond scrolling through the photos on my phone, finally landing on a picture of Bain and I together the last time that he was home.

"I don't think you two look anything alike. Cool tattoos though."

"You're the first to say that, everyone else says we are identical. Maybe you could meet him; he's coming to visit next week."

"I would like that."

Just then, a light breeze swoops through the air, giving me chills, and he wraps his arms around me. I'm not sure what to think of Anthony's affection. I mean, I like him and I like how it feels to be alone and close to him like this. It's just not something I've ever done with someone that's really a stranger. "Has anyone ever told you how beautiful you are?"

I shake my head glancing at him out of the corner of my eye. "Well, they really should, because you are."

Pulling away, I stare at him to make sure he's sincere. "What's wrong?" he asks suddenly.

"Nothing. Its just…Do you do this with a lot of your students?"

"No!" he says firmly, with his forehead creased and an expression I can't quite read on his face. "I told you, if I didn't get to know you I'd always regret it. There's something very special about you. Please don't think I'd do this with anyone else."

CHAPTER 24

-Arion-

I decided if I got Bain drunk, he'd have a better time and be easier to handle at the game. The problem is the man can handle his liquor. He's had three beers and a shot of Patrón and the only difference – he's horny. I'd have to say it was the right decision, though; it's such a turn on to see him like this. If I thought he was horny before, this is a whole new level of eagerness. For the first two quarters of the game, it's been nothing, but dirty talk in my ear. As the cheerleaders clear the floor from their halftime performance, an older gentleman comes over and rests his hand on Bain's shoulder. Bain looks up at him and then immediately stands and the two men embrace.

"Holy shit, how are you, Coach?" he asks.

"Good, good. I think the better question is, how are you?"

"I'm all right."

"How about your parents?"

"My dad's good and my mom's getting there."

"That's great news. It'll take some more time, I'm sure of it. And who's this lovely young lady?" he asks glancing over at me.

"This is my good friend, Arion," he responds.

"Arion, it's a pleasure to meet you. My name is James Lawrence. I coached Bain through high school."

"It's a pleasure to meet you, sir."

"Thank you, but please, just call me Coach."

"Okay, Coach," I respond, looking into his warm, brown eyes.

"You know, Arion, you better start feeding this boy. He has the draft coming up in soon and can't go into it looking like this."

"Funny you should say that. We were just talking about it."

Bain glares at me and I know right away he doesn't want me to push the subject any further. *I'll respect his wishes – for now.*

"Did you hear the news about Conner?" he asks.

Bain shakes his head.

"He tore his ACL, MCL, and meniscus. I believe he's scheduled for surgery this week. From what it sounds like, he's going to heal and try next year's draft.

Bain just nods his head and James watches him, reading his expression. "Do you have any idea what this means for you, son?"

"Coach, I don't know if I—"

He cuts him off and puts his hand up. "Bain, I've

known you since you were fourteen years old, and I know there is no way in the world you would give up on your dreams of the NBA, much less the chance to be a very high draft pick."

The players are back on the court and Coach says, "Call me this week, let's have lunch. I wanna know what's going through your mind, son. Will you at least do that for me?"

"I promise he will," I blurt out and instantly regret it, it's not my place to put Bain on the spot like that. But James doesn't seem like the kind of guy that will let Bain give up on basketball, and I know he needs someone like him.

"It was a pleasure, Arion," he says "Bain, I trust that you'll call me."

He nods his head and we watch James walk off. I lean on Bain's shoulders wrapping my arm around him, feeling guilty for opening my mouth. He looks down at me and kisses the top of my head. Inside I feel bad, I know it wasn't my place to tell James that Bain would call him. However, I could tell that he cares about him and I'm hoping maybe he can talk some sense into him.

The game resumes and I pass him his beer. We watch together, both of us enjoying the intense back and forth battle between these two rivals.

As the teams move from one side of the court to the other, one guy in particular on the opposing team reminds me of Bain. They don't necessarily look alike; they both just carry themselves the same way. "What position did you play?" I ask.

"Guard. Watch number seventeen right here, he's a lot like me."

I smirk at him as he points to the guy I've been watching. He kisses me, holding our mouths together and then asks, "What's so funny?"

"Nothing. I'm not laughing."

"You might not be laughing, but that smirk is all over your face."

"It's always there, silly. Number seventeen, I heard you, and I already had my eye on him."

"You better watch yourself or you're not going to make it out of this arena without a rough fucking," he says strongly into my ear.

"Shhh, I'm focusing." I pretend to ignore him, watching the men on the court. But it pisses him off. Out of the corner of my eye I can see him clear as day, arms crossed and forearms flexing. If I had to guess, my ignoring him is making him a bit jealous.

"Yeah, I definitely like number seventee—"

He cuts me off by yanking me out of my chair. I barely grab my coat, before he begins to rush me away from the court. Guess I didn't get him drunk enough, because he's in total control. Adrenaline surges through me, thinking of what he's going to do. I'm sure he'll take me into a restroom and have his way with me. But as we pass sign after sign, directing us to different bathrooms, he ignores them and heads towards the exit.

"Put your coat on," he snarls.

I comply immediately, just as the brisk air hits me like a ton of bricks. Bain shrugs his coat on and then pulls me tightly against him. Walking to his car, I can't imagine getting undressed in this weather.

"You like number seventeen, do yah?"

I can't help, but giggle at his behavior. I was only watching the guy he told me to, now he's gone all caveman on me, practically dragging me to his car. "You know, number seventeen seems like a great ball handler. Would you mind if I got his jersey? I mean, since you're not going to play again."

He opens my door and ushers me into the car. The intensity in his face makes my pussy tighten. "You're lucky it's cold right now."

"Why?" I ask confused, playing like I don't know what he's thinking.

"Because I would fuck you every which way in my car."

"And you think that I would mind?"

He shakes his head, leaving the parking lot in a hurry. As he exits, I think he'll turn right back towards New Jersey, but instead he goes left and heads into the city. It's only a few blocks 'til he pulls up to The New Yorker, a lavish hotel, and the hot valet guy opens my door.

I look to Bain and he winks at me, then gets out of the car walking around reaching for my hand, making the valet guy feel very small. As our hands connect and we walk in with no luggage, I feel sort of sleazy, but truth be told, Bain turns me on in a way that no other man *ever* has. I would let him fuck me in the middle of this gorgeous lobby with everyone watching if he so desired.

The ceiling is gold and there is a huge, round chandelier hanging from it.

"Welcome to The New Yorker. Are you checking in?" a cute brunette asks.

"We are," Bain responds. "But we don't have reservations."

"I'm sorry, sir, but we're booked for the night. You might try—"

He cuts her off. "You didn't ask what kind of room we wanted. I'd like to book a suite, please." Then he sets down a black American Express card and his ID.

The woman blinks several times, then responds. "Of course, my apologies, sir." She feverishly types away with her cheeks the color of crimson. Bain not only embarrassed but impressed her, and I love it. How dare she judge him and assume what he wants? Doesn't she see the specimen of a man that he is? While we wait, he grabs my neck and whispers in my ear, "We're not staying the night, okay?"

I nod my head, thankful that he remembered. Then the woman hands him the key and says, "I'm so sorry for the misunderstanding. If you need anything at all during your stay, please let us know."

Together, we take the elevator up to the top, all the floors ticking by, one by one. Our room is at the end of the hall and as soon as I enter, I see the view. It's gorgeous and I can't help, but stop and enjoy it. Looking out into the city, I even contemplate staying the night here.

I can sense Bain watching me, then I catch a glimpse of his beautiful, tall reflection in the window as he lets his coat hit the floor, and pulls his tight t-shirt above his head. Next, I hear the metal of his belt and thud of his shoes being kicked off. The noises, combined with his reflection in the dark sky and city lights, depict everything he's doing perfectly. Having him naked like this, I begin undressing myself. I turn towards him, looking at his fully naked body. I love that cock and I begin to strip faster. I make quick work of my clothes, then step to him, dropping to my knees like the first time we met.

I take my hand and wrap it around his gorgeous length, holding it tightly. Squeezing and twisting, I begin with a jerking motion before I twirl my tongue over the end, devouring his pre-cum then go down all the way.

He grunts loudly and pushes his hips towards me, holding the back of my head. I don't stop my movements. I only continue to work him, thankful that I don't have a gag reflex. Moving his hand, he cups my face, holding my cheek. His hair is messy, like it always is. His light eyes pierce right through me, causing me to move that much more.

I whimper at the closeness, then he takes his other

hand and holds the back of my head again. It's like he can't get enough of me, he has to have his hands on me, both of them at all times. I continue watching him 'til his eyes roll back into his head and he loses it, releasing his pent up orgasm and rewarding me with a thick coating of his delicious cum all over my mouth.

He tastes so sweet and light, like no other man I've been with. "Jesus, I'm sorry, beautiful. I couldn't help myself."

"Why are you sorry?" I ask, standing on my feet.

"I didn't mean to come so...soon."

"Don't apologize, that's what tonight's about. I want you to come again and again. There are no time restraints here, it's just us, so let's forget all the rules for once."

I don't know if he caught on or not, but that was my way of saying that I want to stay the night together. I want to be in his arms all night long, looking at this view. I want to fall asleep to the sound of his beating heart and be soothed throughout my sleep by his touch.

"Are you positive?" he asks firmly.

"Yes," I respond grabbing his hand and leading him towards the bed. He follows, holding me around the waist with his free arm, and kisses my shoulder. The moment my knees are pressed against the bed, he pushes me forward. "Scoot up, sexy."

Listening, I turn my head to the side, wanting to get a better look at his tattooed body. As his strong, muscular frame hovers above me, he begins to leave kisses on my mouth, over my cheek, down my neck and back, 'til finally he reaches my butt. Then with a little force, he lifts my body in the air. Making me arch myself up on my knees, giving all of me over to him. He can take me any way he pleases. In this moment, I would let him. But Bain is a gentleman and gently spreads me, so he can sink so sweetly into my pussy. As our flesh connects, I moan and he growls. He fills me with his thick member and I love how he's still horny for me. His cock is rock hard and I settle back down letting his weight push me into the mattress. He reaches for my hands and interlocks our fingers, pulling my arms far beside me, then parts my legs in a similar manner. I'm spread below him like an X. My breathing is harsh and ragged, truly wanting everything he's willing to give me tonight.

With slow, calculated movements, he pulls and pushes himself inside of me, causing my body to burn from head to toe. Every ounce of me needs this. I know this isn't the first time Bain and I have had sex, but it feels like the first time we've really connected. I've only ever experienced this connection with one other person and to feel this again is so enlivening. With deep breaths, I begin to moan Bain's name.

"Fuck…say it, A," he grunts into my ear with a deep voice, pushing himself even farther inside of me.

I repeat it over and over again, letting the cries of passion take me far away from this world. He never picks up speed or moves with urgency. Finally, he lets go of my hands and pushes off of my back. I rest up on my elbows and then he pulls out of me, flipping me over and in the blink of an eye, he's nuzzled himself back inside. With my eyes tightly shut, I wrap my legs around him and do my best to meet his every thrust.

His noises are such a fucking turn-on, they're so deep and low. I can't help but listen to him closely and get lost to him in this moment. Looking at Bain, he is in his zone, eyes closed, forehead creased, and lost in us.

"So sweet," he whispers, a phrase that only Nate has ever said to me. Instantly, his face flashes before my eyes and I can't help, but grab each of Bain's ass cheeks, holding them firmly. The moment I make contact holding him like this, Nate is gone, and before me, only Bain, sexier than ever. In that moment, I realize maybe God brought him into my life for a reason. I'll never get Nate back. I know that and I need to let him go. Maybe Bain *is* who I'm truly meant to be with?

Bain leans down, connecting our mouths, and I give him all of me. I turn over every single ounce of the woman that I am to this gorgeous man. As we kiss and fuck, he holds me firmly, coming inside of me. On cue, my body lets go along with his. Our tongues thrashing against one another's, only intensifies every sensation.

Spirals and bliss, sprinkled with ecstasy, give me the most delicious orgasm ever. Once his movements slow, he begins to get off of me, but I stop him.

He looks down at me confused; we've never stayed

connected like this before. "Are you ready to get going?" he asks.

I shake my head and wrap my arms around him, holding our bodies together. "No, let's stay."

Bain settles for a few moments, then looks down at me and says, "Arion, I don't want to be the cause of any regrets for you."

Smiling, I kiss him, and then pull him to lay his head back down on me. "You won't."

"I mean it. You mean too much to me to risk staying the night together."

"Will you just be quiet and enjoy this moment?" I ask.

He nods his head on my chest and I gently rake my fingernails up and down his back. His skin, so soft and warm. My touch causes his dick to harden again inside of me.

"You're an animal," I tease him.

"I have to get my five hundred dollars worth of use out of this room. I know my dad is going to chew my ass later for this one, but it was so worth it."

CHAPTER 25

-Bain-

With Arion wrapped in my arms, all of my worries are suppressed to the back of my mind. The clock on the nightstand reads 10:47am. I know we have to check out at 11:00, but I can't wake her. I just can't. I'm still shocked that she stayed the night with me, and I fear deep down that this is going to change everything.

Even though she said it wouldn't, I'm worried that it will. I've been up for over an hour, my mind racing over all the events that have taken place recently. And it all comes down to the fact that I have to make a decision. I'm almost twenty-three years old and Arion is right. Do I want to look back and be in the NBA or still in this rut? I can hear Kinsey now; she would be pissed at me for acting this way. Sometimes, I guess I just need a kick in the ass to put things in perspective and to fight for justice for Kinsey. I know I don't want to live with regrets any longer; it's something I've been wallowing in, a sickening, horrible feeling that I never want to experience again.

Arion stirs awake next to me. I release my grip on her warm, perfect body, allowing her to stretch. I watch a little scared, like the moment her eyes open she's gonna freak out, but that moment never comes. Instead she rolls into me and wraps her arms around me. "What time is it?" she asks.

"Almost eleven," I respond in a calm, even tone.

"Do we have to go soon?"

"Uh-huh."

"I don't wanna leave here."

"Why?" I ask as she finally looks up at me, her eyes as clear as the ocean water.

"I love the city. Just something about it feels like home."

"Why don't you live here?"

"We don't all have crazy money like you, Bain."

"I don't have crazy money. My parents do."

"Well, regardless, it would be far from you."

"And that's a problem for you now?"

She nods her head and my heart tightens at her affection. For the first time since I've know her, I feel like she truly cares about me, and more than just as a casual fuck. I've known all along that she's wanted me, but not like this.

Lying together with our legs interlocked and arms bound around each other's naked bodies, I can truly say I've never felt this content with anyone. Basketball was always my priority, but Arion could be that, now.

I shake my head to clear those thoughts. Just because we stayed the night together doesn't mean things are going to be any different and one comment from her certainly doesn't change anything, or mean that she wants anything more than a fuck buddy. "I gotta pee," she says sitting up. The sheets fall off her breasts before she gets up and walks into the bathroom stark naked and white as ivory. My cock tingles watching her leave. *She's so fucking hot.* I hate that it's close to 11. *Damn it.* I would fuck her like an animal if we didn't have to check out, but it's time to go. Getting out of bed, I find my clothes in a pile by the expansive wall of glass windows and begin to dress.

Arion emerges and asks, "Do we really have to go?"

"Yeah, look at the time. Besides, don't you have work today?"

"Oh shit, I have to be there at noon."

I can't help, but laugh at her as she scrambles to get dressed.

"Why don't you just call in?"

"No way, I'm the boss. I'll just be a little late. You think I could work in these clothes?" she asks.

"Fuck no," I blurt out as she looks at me in her skin-tight, white jeans.

"You're right, let's go."

We fly out of the hotel and get the car from the valet. Thankfully, we're at the right time to miss the really heavy traffic. But it's New York, so it's never really light.

I make the drive in great time and pull up to Arion's in

just under an hour.

"I'll call you tonight," she says, leaning over and kissing me quickly on the lips. But I can't let her go that fast and I hold her face, keeping our mouths together a moment longer. She looks at me smiling before hopping out of my car and I watch until she's safely inside. I hate to pull away, but I have to.

Once I'm home, I enter and the noise of the TV catches me off guard. ESPN is doing coverage for the upcoming draft. As I read the scroll bar on the side, it says *Conner out, will Adams be the top point guard?* Anxiously I sit down, waiting for the broadcast to get to my story. The announcers go over Conner's injury and then debate if I'll be the top point guard in the draft.

One of the announcers talks about how he thinks I don't have a chance and that I'll fall in the draft considering I haven't played in the past few months. The other has a different opinion though, going on about the raw talent I possess and how you never lose that. Then they show a reel of highlight clips from some of my best games. Watching myself on the screen is something I haven't seen in a while and it…excites me.

God, I really miss the game. I miss the guys and the camaraderie we shared when we played the game at such a high level. I miss the roar of the crowds and how my body felt the next day; bone tired and completely satisfied that I'd played my heart out. It was the best. I listen intently, happy inside that watching myself sparks something – I do still fucking give a shit. It's always been my dream, and for a short period of time I turned my back on it. But I think I now know what I have to do. As the debate ends and the guys never bring up Kinsey or why I've been out, I think I might have a shot at this.

Pulling my phone out, I make the call Arion promised I would. James answers right away. "I always knew you wouldn't let this dream go."

"Don't jump ahead of yourself. Maybe I called to tell you I'm not interested," I retort back at him.

"Come on, Bain, this is a once in a lifetime opportunity. You know this is what Kinsey would want you to do." Hearing him bring her back up and how *she* would want me to do it, brings a weight over my body. Grief instantly replaces the thoughts that I could play ball again. Even though it would disappoint her, I'm not ready. there's still so much that is going on, I just don't think I can do this right now.

"Bain, are you there? Can you hear me?"

"Yeah…I'm here. Sorry. Listen can I call you later?"

"Nope, there's no need for that. I'll see you in an hour at the Jefferson Four-Forty for lunch."

"James, I don't think I can get there today."

"You can and you will. Don't bullshit me, son. Did you see the news?"

"Yeah, I did," I grumble, hating to be spoken to like a rebellious teen. I guess it is a bit my fault for calling him.

"So you're coming then?"

I agree to go, because it's only a conversation and James is just trying to help. He's always wanted what's best for me and maybe he can help me figure out just what that is. Plus for a brief moment, watching myself play sparked something inside of me. We hang up and I head into the restroom, looking at my blank expression in the mirror.

Instinctively, I pull open the drawer that contains all of my pill bottles. Jesus Christ, I'm a goddamn mess. I really don't have time for that shit, but I can't get through this conversation sober. I know if I do this and agree to get back into basketball, I'll have to be done with these forever. But I'll worry about that then. Fuck, maybe I can make it through the day on just this one pill and then dwindle the cravings down slowly over the next few days. Opening my drawer, I take a Hydro.

Checking the time on my watch, I hop in the shower and change, not wasting a second to allow myself to change my mind, before jumping back in the car. The Four-Forty is a bit of a drive from my house, so I text James and let him know that with traffic, I'm running a bit late. He texts back that he's already got us a table.

Parking out front, I take a shaky breath and hope this is something I can do. I've come this far. Walking inside, I see his salt-n-pepper hair right away, then his smile.

He stands as I approach and proceeds to hug me. "It's good to see you, son."

"Same to you, Coach," I respond as he passes me his cell phone, showing me a text that reads, *Do you think you can get me an interview with Adams?*

"Who's that from?" I ask as we both sit down.

"Yahoo Sports. An old friend of mine saw us talking at the game last night."

I shake my head and place my face in my hands. This is unreal, absolutely unreal.

"Bain, I know you're not feeling like your heart's in it anymore, but I can't let you turn your back on this. This is too big of an opportunity."

"I know," I respond staring into my lap, picking at the rough fabric of my jeans.

"Listen, I wanna manage you. I don't want you to pay me or anything. I just want to see you succeed and ultimately watch you be happy, knowing I had a part in it."

"But what if I don't make it, or I'm not the same on the court anymore?"

"You will be. I know for a fact, son, raw talent of your degree doesn't change. Yeah, you'll be a little rusty, but a few weeks of workouts and you'll be back to how you were."

"If we do this, do I have to go back to school?"

"No," he firmly replies. "You have enough credits to graduate. Guys join the NBA all the time after a few years of college."

"How do you know so much about me?"

"You've always been my favorite kid. I've kept tabs on you over the years and after your sister passed, I made sure that you leaving school wouldn't impact your degree. I've always known the NBA would want you, I just didn't know they would project you to get drafted so high."

"I can't believe that's what they are saying."

"I know, but with Conner out, you're it. Your time's now, Bain."

"Damn. Okay. I hear all that you're saying, I really do. I do feel I wanna give it a try, but I need to see how I feel on the court."

"I can get you into a few pick-up games."

"Fuck no," I blurt out, "Not if everyone has their eyes on me. Not yet anyways. Let's get some practice in first, let me shake the rust off."

"I was hoping you were going to say that. I talked to Damian Millani – you remember him, don't you?"

My mind flashes back to the seven-foot-tall ex-NBA all-star himself. "How could I not remember him? He's a legend."

"He a very good friend of mine. He said if we're interested he's happy to let us use his private gym."

Staring at James point blank, I simply ask him, "How did you set all this up? I mean, what if I would've said no?"

"I'm methodical, and I knew you wouldn't let me down. Come on, let's get going."

"What about lunch?" I complain.

"That's right, you do need to put some weight back on."

James calls the waiter over and we both order burgers. Then spend far too much time reminiscing. Going back reminds me why I love the game so much, and James too. He really molded me into the player that I am today.

Driving back home after one hell of a day of practice, I can't help the smile that's on my face. It's ear to ear and I've never felt better. Well, if it weren't for the nagging background noise of my body starting to wear down from not having any pills. But my shooting from within the paint was ninety percent and my free throws were on fire. My phone rings and the screen shows it's a private number.

"Hello," I answer.

"Bain, sweetie, is everything okay?" my mother asks in a panicked tone.

"Yeah, of course mom, why?

"It's your dad. I can't get a hold of him."

"Come on, Mom, you know how busy he is. I'm sure he's been in meetings or something."

"I don't know, Bain. I have a bad feeling."

"I'll talk to him soon and tell him to answer next time you call whether he's busy or not. I promise he's been good. Just working a lot."

"Okay, thank you, dear. I'm sorry to call in such a tizzy. It's just...I...I can't have anything happen to my guys."

"It won't. I promise we're good. How have you been?"

"Good, really good. I'm starting to feel like myself. How 'bout you? What have you been up to?"

"Not much. I actually practiced some basketball today with Coach Lawrence."

"Oh my God, honey, that's great news. How was it? How did you get in touch with him?"

"I ran into him at a Knicks game the other night."

"Really? Who did you go with?" she asks surprised. I know why her tone is the way it is. Although she was a drunk for the last six months, she knew I was in a slump and had pushed all of my friends away.

Should I tell her about Arion?

"Uhh, just a friend."

"Bain…"

Her tone is long and drawn out, reminding me of the way she used to get when Kinsey and I would get in trouble.

"It's just a girl, Mom."

"Really, just a girl?

"Yeah, really.

"Bain, you haven't dated a girl in months. If you're spending your time with one now and getting back into basketball, something has happened."

"Time's up, Renee," I faintly hear a woman in the background say.

"I gotta go, sweetie. You should bring her down here.

I wanna meet this girl."

"We'll see. Goodbye, Mom. I love you."

"Love you, son. Bye," she says and we hang up.

Not only hearing my mom's voice, but hearing her in such good spirits, makes today one of the best days I've had in a long time — a really, really long time.

CHAPTER 26

-Kinsey-

"Do you want another glass of wine?" Anthony asks me.

"Are you trying to get me drunk?"

"Never," he says pouring me another glass without waiting for my response. I smirk at him, sipping on the deliciousness that he's serving me.

"What is this?"

"It's a Pink Moscato. You like it?"

"I love it."

"Good. So tell me, what are your goals after you graduate?"

Staring into the corner of the room, I contemplate his question. What are my goals after I graduate?

"I really don't know. Jesus, that sounds horrible. I don't have a plan for my life yet."

"It's not horrible; you're young. I felt that way at one point too, but I discovered that I had a talent and I could share that with emerging photographers like you. What do you like to photograph?"

"Don't laugh, okay?"

"Never, this is your life we're talking about."

"Sports. My brother plays basketball and I love taking pictures at his games. It honestly doesn't matter the sport though, just catching the action in the moment is amazing."

"I love it."

CHAPTER 27

-Arion-

"Starbucks, this is Arion."

"Hey, you're still working."

"Uhhh, yeah," I respond in a sharp tone.

"I've been trying to get a hold of you on your cell phone." Suddenly I recognize the voice. It's Bain on the other end and my insides calm. Hearing him worried about me makes all the stress of this crazy day wash away.

"Sorry, I didn't recognize your voice. It's crazy loud in here. I didn't charge my phone last night because someone kept me out all night. So it...ummm...died." I keep counting the money in the register and almost come undone with his next comment.

"You won't need your phone tonight either."

"Why is that?"

"You'll see. What time are you leaving?"

Glancing at the clock it's 8:46pm. We close at ten and it's already slowed down. "I think I'll leave around nine."

"Cool. See you soon, then," he responds and hangs

up.

There's an unfamiliar excited tone to his voice, something that I'm not used to, but I like it. Knowing that it's not long 'til I see Bain, I wrap up the deposit, ever so thankful that it's not busy anymore.

"What's up with the smile?" Sasha asks me as I come out of the office.

"What do you mean?" I look at her with a scowl on my face. "I've been smiling all day."

"Haaahhh!" she blurts out, causing a few customers to look in our direction.

"You are such a bag. We we're busy today and I was stressed, okay? I'm leaving now, since I was off, I don't know, four hours ago."

"You do that," she quips back. "And make sure you keep that smile with you."

"Suck it, bag." I rip my apron off jokingly and snatch my purse before exiting.

"What's a bag?" she questions as I push the door open with my back. I point at her and she just shakes her head.

The fresh air feels amazing, like my lungs have been deprived all day. Sparking up a cigarette, I hop in my car, pull out of the lot, and speed to see Bain. I know he didn't say he would be there, but I know he will. That's just how he is, and sure enough, as I pull up in front of my apartment, there he is. Backed into a parking spot, messy hair and light eyes gleaming at me. He's got my signature smirk plastered on his face as I pull up next to him.

Flicking my cigarette out, I pop a piece of gum and exit. My stomach is a mess, a mix of butterflies and adrenaline, so new and different than when I was with Nate.

"You need to quit smoking," he says.

I can't help but laugh at him.

"I mean it, A."

"Fine, I'll think about it," I respond, glancing at him as he pulls me tightly to him. I don't get very long to look into those eyes because he quickly nuzzles himself into my neck. "God, you smell good."

"I smell like coffee."

Shaking his head he says, "Not right here." And nuzzles my neck again.

I hold him tight, loving how even when I feel gross, he makes me feel so sexy. "Come on. Let's head in, so you can change."

"Do you really think I need to change, or can I just get naked?"

He looks up, like he is contemplating what I'm saying. "Fine. Naked."

With a firm squeeze to my ass, we head inside. Aubrey is sitting on the couch painting her toenails. The last time she did that, she got more polish on her skin than her nails.

"Hey, guys," she says and barely looks at us.

"Hey, girl. I'm gonna shower real quick."

She nods her head with her tongue stuck out, obviously in deep concentration. Bain and I glance at each other and smile. We walk into my room and I shut the door, turning to find him sprawled across my bed. "You okay?" I ask as I begin getting undressed.

"I'm good. I'm tired, but good."

"What did you do today?" I ask.

"Are you sure you're ready for it?"

"Uhhh, yeah. Why wouldn't I be?"

"Just checking. Remember James from the game last night? I met him for lunch. We talked about a lot of stuff, about me giving my NBA dreams another chance. Then he took me to an ex-pro's private home gym and I worked out for most of the afternoon."

Thinking about his words, I wonder why he went to somebody's house to work out. "Arion, you have no idea how great it felt to get back on the court."

"Holy shit, you didn't tell me you played basketball!"

"Well, what did you think I did?"

"You said 'worked out.'"

"That's what we call it."

I sit next to him, naked, barely able to contain my excitement. He senses just how happy I am for him and pulls me on top of him.

"I can't thank you enough for giving me the drive to do it. Your words kept replaying in my head today, over and over. And I knew every time I heard them, what I wanted to do. What would really make me happy. It was a battle long overdue and I knew the minute James and I began talking, that I was meant to follow my dreams."

Crashing my lips against his, I get lost in Bain, in who he is, what we have, and what he gives me. There's a sense of security about him and knowing that I helped him continue following his dreams, makes me feel proud. With his hands tight around my body, we lie there together, enjoying each other.

"I'm so proud of you."

"It's all because of you. Thank you for motivating me."

"Anytime."

"Wanna shower?" he asks.

"Please," I respond, and he lifts me in his arms, carrying me into the bathroom. He sets me on my feet and turns the water on. I can't take my eyes off of him as he undresses. He's so tall and muscular and...mine.

We step into the hot water, letting it cascade down our bodies. Leaning my head back, I drench my long, blonde hair knowing he is watching my every move. With his head tilted down looking at me intently, water beads off the tip of his nose, and some rolls down his oh-so-plump lips.

He catches me off guard as I run my hands through my hair. He separates my pussy, touching the inside of my already swollen lips, as he moves his fingers in a circular motion. He's giving me the right amount of pleasure and I almost jump from the sensation. Looking at him, his eyes are watching exactly what he's doing, and without speaking, he drops to his knees. I step forward so the water doesn't pelt him and brace my weight on the square tiles of the shower.

He grips my ass and sucks my clit, swirling his tongue over it so gently. I moan, giving in to the desire, and close my eyes. Bain's very patient in what he's doing. The pleasure's so great, I instantly want to come, but I fight the feeling, keeping myself focused on not letting go.

We stay like this, in this moment and position, until I cannot take anymore. My noises show him what he's doing to me, and I pull away looking down at him as he still stares at my sex. Reaching for his hand, I guide him up. He stands, and I reach between us, gripping his hard cock with more force than he showed me. I rub him against my sensitive pussy, stroking him at the same time.

Bain makes the sexiest noises when he's turned on. I love that I can do that to him. Suddenly, he pushes my hand away and takes ahold of his massive cock, guiding himself inside of me. Slowly filling me, both of our eyes watch the contact of our bodies molding into one.

Taking my arms, I reach up and brace myself on his forearms. Leaning away from me, he holds my hips and moves at a gentle pace. Not fast or forceful – just right.

His size confounds me, just like his endurance. Leaning my head back, I close my eyes, shutting out the world and everything else in the process. My breaths are short, enjoying this bliss. Then out of nowhere and without warning, Bain explodes inside of me. A warm surge of cum fills me, followed by his thrusts and my body finds its own release. So strong, quaking from the tips of my hair to the bottoms of my feet. Leaning into Bain, I scream into his skin.

As possessively as ever, he holds me to him. I grip him back, never before experiencing a feeling quite like this.

It's been a rough few days. After Bain's first practice, he got sick. I've never seen anyone with the flu so bad and I am so thankful that he is finally feeling better. Plus, we got an update from the FBI that they have a suspect on their radar. Bain's dad didn't know much when he called and I didn't probe Bain. I was too worried about him feeling so bad that I didn't want to make things worse by asking a ton of questions. I know it tore him up inside because even though he was in and out of sleep for the better part of three days, he kept checking his phone and asking when he woke up, if I'd heard anything. Driving into New York, I ask him, "So what is a pick-up game anyways?"

"It's really just a high-energy game with the top local guys," he says kissing my knuckles and then lays our intertwined hands back on his lap.

"Have you played in a lot of them?"

"I used to, all the time. But I haven't for quite a while."

"Will there be a lot of people there?"

"Probably. I mean, there will be people there to see the game. And now since James is managing me, he called in a few scouts. He said there are a lot of people wanting to see me play."

I don't ask any more questions, as I'm anxious not only for Bain, but for me. "Can I have a cigarette?" I ask Bain.

"Come on, A, you've done so well these last few days. Here, have another piece of gum."

I scowl at him as he passes it to me. "I don't get how you can just expect me to stop smoking."

"You can do it. You've done so well already. Plus, we're here; this should keep your mind off of cigarettes for a bit." Bain puts the car in park and I look at the fenced in court. It's lined so densely with people that I can't even make out the players.

"Stick with James, okay? And for me, try not to smoke."

I nod my head, loving how controlling he's been over smoking, and exit the car. Bain and I meet at the front, and right away he grips my hand tightly as I scan the crowd looking for James, who is nowhere to be seen. Then suddenly, he's standing right next to us.

The two guys hug and I shake his hand, listening as they talk. "I only committed you to one game. I didn't want to push anything since you've been sick."

"That's cool with me."

"Are you feeling better and keeping food down?"

"Yeah, I feel good. Thanks for being concerned."

"Good, 'cause you're up next and there are scouts from the Knicks, Pistons, and Nets, so don't hold back. Play like you know how, so we can get you the best possible deal."

Bain kisses me, holding my head firmly in his hands for a moment. I indulge in him, loving how sweet he's been while sick, then upon opening my eyes, I see a few lights flash out of the corner of my eye and look to see that we are being photographed. "Sorry, A," he whispers.

"It's okay. Now go kick some ass. I'm excited I finally get to see you in action."

James and I watch him jog off. He then takes his sweats off, exposing his hot tattooed legs. We proceed at our own walking pace to a small section on the risers, where the front row is open and we sit down. "So things with you two are serious?" James asks me.

I take a moment and think about his question, watching Bain stretch on the court. I couldn't tell you how we got here, or why I feel the way I do, but yeah we're definitely serious. "He's the second most serious boyfriend I've had."

"Are you prepared to answer questions about your past and what happened with Nathaniel?"

I almost spin in my seat to look James in the face. Is he fucking serious? "Please, don't take offence to what I'm saying, Arion. I have to look out for Bain right now. Everything needs to be covered, we can't have anything compromise his future."

"And I understand that, but how is my past any of his future employer's business?"

"I'm just saying the question could come up, and if it does, I want you to be prepared. These teams are investing not only millions, but sometimes years if they pick the wrong kid."

"I'm the last person you have to be worrying about. You really need to talk to Bain soon regarding how he is going to handle being drilled about how much time he spent out of school and everything with Kinsey."

"I will, I will," James says.

The referee blows the whistle bringing both our eyes to the court. The two teams stand in the middle, both of the tallest players ready to tip the ball in their team's direction. Then the ref throws the ball up in that air and it gets tipped to Bain. He catches it like his hands have glue on them and he dribbles the ball down the court with natural confidence. I watch his eyes and how he looks for a teammate to pass the ball to. Then he gets an open opportunity to drive the ball to the hoop, and goes for the rim. Making his move into the paint, he looks like a man amongst boys, dunking the ball cleanly. The way his body moves through the air, is effortless. He turns to jog up the court looking only at me for a brief moment with a smile and a wink. I can't help, but have a huge grin on my face, jumping to my feet and cheering like a maniac.

CHAPTER 28

-Bain-

I feel bad for leaving Arion waiting as long as I did after the game, but with my impressive performance today, everyone wanted to talk with me. I'm surprised that I did so well considering how sick I've been over the last few days. I guess this is one time in my life that I'm grateful for getting the flu. It sounds weird to say, but I was so sick, that there was nothing I could do except lay around and throw up. That also meant that I didn't take any pills. I wanted to stop anyways, so this just made me do it without the internal back and forth struggle in my own mind. I can't tell you how good it feels to be level-headed again and not have anything clouding my judgment.

Finally, I say goodbye to James and head towards Arion, waiting in my car. *Fuck, please don't let her be pissed.* I mean, if there was something that I could have done to get out of here more quickly, I would have.

Getting in the driver's seat of my car, I see she is curled up into a tiny ball and looks as comfy as ever. I know she is tired — these last few days have stressed her like they have me. When I close the door, even though I do my best to stay quiet, she looks at me. "Hey, I'm sorry it took so long."

"Don't be. I would've stayed by your side, but I'm exhausted. I knew coming today that it was an all-day thing. So it's all good."

"Thank you," I respond, leaning in and kissing her soft forehead as she stays in her comfy ball. "Let's get you home and to bed, beautiful." Pulling the car out, we begin the long haul out of the city and back into Jersey.

"How did it feel to be back on the court, in a real game?" she asks me.

Loosening my grip on the wheel, I think back over the game for a few beats.

"Well, while you're lost in your daydream—"

"I'm not lost," I cut her off. "Don't ever tell a man he's lost, okay? I was just reminiscing."

We both bust out laughing and I realize how horrible I sounded saying *reminiscing.*

"You keep daydreaming, my basketball star."

Reaching over, she touches my thigh. I love her hands. I love her touch. I'll take it anyway that I can get it. Very softly, she rubs my leg through my shorts, back and forth, and the inappropriate beast inside of me wants to pull over and fuck her 'til she can't handle it any longer, but I stink and I won't do that to her. What I will do is drive us safely to her house then have my way with her all night long.

I park at Arion's where everything is silent; the sun has set and there aren't many people out tonight. We head inside and I'm anxious to fuck her. Hopefully, we'll be alone.

"Aubrey," Arion shouts as we enter the apartment. The house is quiet and she goes towards her room. "She's not here."

"Then I have you all to myself," I say and drag her to the bathroom, tearing my sweaty basketball clothes off on the way. She giggles behind me and begins undressing herself.

"Fuck yeah, get naked for me," I growl watching her remove her clothing. "Let me see that perfect body of yours." My cock is instantly rock hard and dripping with cum. As she steps to me, I show more force than I mean to, but she doesn't falter. My girl likes a little pain crossed in with her pleasure.

"Tell me what you want," I ask, dragging my tongue down her neck. Her scent is a drug to me. There's something so erotic about it that I almost go all caveman on her when I press my nose hard against any part of her.

"I…" she trails off.

"Tell me," I snap.

"I want you."

"You have me. I'm right here."

She shakes her head, loosening her hold on me. I know right away that I've done something or said something I shouldn't have.

"I won't always have you, though."

My heart drops hearing her say those words. *What? NO! Why?* "Don't say things like that, I'm not going anywhere."

She laughs awkwardly, and the noise is a hard blow to my ego. "You don't even know where you're going to get drafted. What happens if you end up in California?"

"Then we'll move there. I don't give a shit what you say, I'm not going anywhere without you. I'm in this for the long haul."

"So was Nate," she whispers. Hearing the words makes all the pieces click into place. "Plus, I can't leave my job. I've worked too hard to get this store."

"Arion, you can transfer, and do you think he had a choice?"

"He did. He didn't need to join the Marines."

"That's true, but I'm sure he did it to secure a future for the both of you. He wouldn't have done it knowing that it would have kept you apart."

Tilting my head to get a good look at her, I can see the pain. Not knowing what to do in that moment, I wrap her in my hold, pressing our naked bodies as closely together as I can. My cock aches wanting to be inside of her. I don't need to move, or come, or do anything else, but just enjoy the closeness. So I nudge myself against her opening and like a good girl, she accepts me.

Taking my time, I slowly ease my way all the way in. Nestled in her to the hilt, she pulls away trying to get some friction. Who am I kidding? I can't be inside of her without moving, so I appease her efforts and comply, but still only moving slowly. Being inside of her always sets me on fire, whether I am going as slow as this, or fucking her madly.

I need to take care of her, so I walk us to the bed and lie down with my feet still hanging off the edge. She keeps her eyes closed as her hair hits the mattress like a puff of wind. I lean up, taking one last look at what is the perfection of her body beneath mine, before I unleash the animal that's inside. It's been knocking at the door all day, watching her cheer me on. If it wasn't for her, pushing me, I don't know that I would have given basketball another try.

"God, Bain," she cries gripping my forearms. Looking down, my muscles and tattoos tighten under her hold. My movements are now urgent. I have my weight braced above her, my hands balled into fists, allowing me to move effortlessly inside of her.

"Jesus, A, your cunt."

She moans, locking her feet behind my back, the friction just as much her demise as it is mine, causing us to simultaneously combust together. The moment I let go, my orgasm is so intense, like nothing I've ever experienced. Hers is just as good. I can tell because as soon as I look at her, she is panting – struggling to catch her breath.

The pleasure fades away and I can't help, but laugh at her with her nails still dug into my arms.

"You okay?" I ask.

"I'm more than okay."

Leaning down, I leave a kiss on her salty chest and then hop off. She follows suit and we get into the shower together. She doesn't bring up the fact that I asked her to move with me if I get drafted. I know she's worried about her job, but there's got to be a thousand Starbucks across the US that she could transfer to. Deep down, I know if I go, she'll go, she has to. We can't be apart.

Neither of us is a person of many words, but when they are needed, we express them. After our shower, I put on a pair of sweats I take from my duffel bag and watch her dry off. Lying on the bed, she's observing my body and asks, "What made you get all these tattoos?"

"Life. I don't know, I've always been into ink. You like them, don't you?"

"A lot," she responds, and leans down, kissing my hand then leaves a trail up one of my arms. My phone rings, interrupting our exchange, and she stops, knowing that I have to answer it.

"I'm sorry."

She sits next to me as I grab it out of my shorts from the floor.

"Bain." My father's tone is panicked.

"What's up, Dad?"

"Jesus Christ, Bain." He's sobbing, his words are barely coherent.

"Dad," I shout into the receiver. "What's wrong?"

"Are you okay?" he asks.

"Yeah, of course! Why?"

He tries to regain his composure. "The news, turn on the fucking news."

I turn wildly in Arion's room searching for the remote. Then, once it's in my hand, I flip the TV on and search for a news station. The second I see the screen, everything I've worried about over the last eight months hits me like a ton of bricks.

The news reporter is standing in front of a seaside home and says, "The FBI made the arrest of Anthony Eldridge today." They show a mid-twenties male with his head hung low being walked out of the home in handcuffs. I don't recognize him at all. "He's being charged with the kidnapping and first-degree murder of Kinsey Adams. She was a young student who passed away late last year. Her death was originally ruled as a suicide, however, since day one, that's been a mystery to those closest to her. Her brother, Bain Adams, quoted her as 'a loving free sprit that would never hurt a fly, much less herself.'" Hearing the reporter quote my words, which I barely remember saying, makes it feel like she left so long ago. "Detective Mark Eldridge, the accused's uncle, was also arrested. He was the lead investigator on the case and is being held on felony menacing charges. Detective Eldridge is believed to have helped Anthony cover up the entire ordeal. It's a tragic day for many in the great state of New Jersey. I'm Rebecca Zalapois, reporting for Channel 3 News."

The phone is gone, I don't know where it is. All I can see in that moment is Arion's face and I say to her. "She didn't do it, A. She didn't fucking kill herself."

She nods her head, as a mix of emotions rush through me. My heart is racing, and for the first time in God only knows how long, I can breathe. "Fuck, my dad." Looking on the ground for the phone, I find it, picking it back up, asking, "Dad?"

"I'm here, son. You were right all along – she didn't do it."

He sounds a lot calmer than he did before. I think giving him some time to process the information helped. I'm not sure how finding out someone was murdered versus killing themselves could make a difference like this, but for us it does. In one way it doesn't make a difference – she's still not ever coming back. But knowing that she didn't choose to leave us relieves a lot of the what-ifs.

"No, she didn't. Do you recognize the guy?"

"No. Do you?" he asks me.

"Not at all, he doesn't look one bit familiar."

"Why would someone kill her?" I ask. It pains me to think someone could so heartlessly take her life.

"There are a lot of sick people in this world, son. Some of them we will never understand."

"I guess you're right. I knew all along that piece of shit detective was crooked."

"I just don't have a clue why in God's name a man of his stature would cover up such a heinous crime."

"Because they are family. It sickens me, Dad. I hope they throw the fucking book at him like the piece of shit he is."

"I know, I hope so too,"

"Does Mom know yet?"

"No. I'm going to call up there now. Would you and Arion want to make a visit with me this weekend to see her? I'm sure after finding out, she could use some family time."

"I'll ask Arion if she has to work, but I'm sure we can make it happen. What about the FBI? Have they or anyone else contacted you?"

"No." Just then I hear his doorbell ring. "Hang on. It's them, son. I'll call you later."

"Are you sure? I can come over there now."

"No, no." The doorbell rings again. "I'm gonna run."

We hang up and I look at Arion. She opens her arms to me and I lay my head on her lap, loving the strength she gives me. She runs those talented fingers through my hair and whispers, "Bain, I'm so sorry. I can't even begin to tell you how sorry I am."

"Just hold me for now."

CHAPTER 29

-Kinsey-

"Do you want to sit out back?"

"It's freezing!" I slur, feeling the effects of the alcohol.

He hands me a blanket, not caring that I complained about the weather, and I snatch it out of his hand.

"I'll start a fire in the pit. It will help keep you warm."

I get up, agreeing to get some fresh air, ultimately hoping it will clear my mind. Anthony grabs my wine glass and we proceed outside. The view of the ocean is breathtaking and the sounds of the waves crashing in instantly consume me.

Sitting on the love seat, I pull my legs under me and put the soft blanket over my cold body. All of a sudden, the fire pit in front of me starts and I look at Anthony. He walks away from a panel of switches as the automatic covers on the sides of the patio are lowered. The lights dim, and soft music croons through the speakers. He hands me back my glass, which is already full, and I want to protest, but the wine is delicious. Staring into his eyes, he is delicious too. Taking the blanket, he lifts the corner and slides underneath it with me.

I cross one leg over the other turning my entire torso towards him. "You're so gorgeous," he whispers into my ear. I moan, not only at his words, but loving the attention. "Can I kiss you?" he asks.

"Please."

The moment I speak the word, our mouths are connected. Hot, wet tongues, tangled kisses.

My wine glass is outstretched in my hand and he takes it from me. Then he leans me back, pressing our bodies together as we kiss. I'm not sure if it's the alcohol or not, but I want him. He runs his hand up my body from my hip to my breast and massages it through the fabric of my clothing. His touch sends shivers through me. I want more. Spreading my legs, I wrap them around him. His erection is hard, and he grinds it into me, saying, "God, I want to feel you."

Kissing him back, I want to feel him as well. Then a wave of dizziness takes over. I must have had too much wine. However, my vision blurs beyond the normal and as I go to move my arms, I can't. I'm immobile beneath him. He looks down at me like he's watching what is happening and says, "Yes, that's it. Let it take you over, baby. I'm going to have fun with you tonight."

My skin crawls at his words and I want to scream. But that is gone too; I can't. My voice doesn't work. Long blinks take over and then a very scary darkness...

CHAPTER 30

-*Arion*-

This has been one of the craziest weeks of my life. First finding out that Bain's sister was murdered, then the media got wind of that, and the fact that we were dating, put my face on TV. Now I'm on the way to meet his mom, while she's in rehab of all places. It's been a triple whammy, that's for sure. Thankfully, Bain agreed that we both needed some time away, so we're going to stay in Virginia for a few days after we see Renee. My eyes feel heavy on the drive and I let myself drift.

"We're almost there, sleepyhead," he whispers, rubbing my cheek with his thumb and forefinger.

I moan a little in protest. I swear I only closed my eyes for a minute, but it had to have been a lot longer. "I can keep driving if you'd rather."

I shake my head and reach down to adjust my seat, letting it put me back into a seated position.

Glancing around us, I pull my bearings together, trying to figure out just where we are. Nothing looks familiar.

The roads are skinny and lined with low trees. "Did you sleep well?" he asks me.

"I barely slept," I protest.

"A, check the clock, babe. We left at seven this morning." He started calling me "babe" last night and I like it. No one has ever called me that before. Nate always called me "A." And other than those two, I've never let anyone into my heart. "Holy hell, I did sleep for a long time. Why didn't you wake me?"

"You needed the rest."

"That's such bullshit. I could see an hour, but Jesus Christ, Bain, it's been five."

He chuckles at my fit, cocking one eyebrow at me and says, "Are you done?"

"I guess."

"Good. So my dad's grabbing us lunch for our visit. Do you need anything before we get there?"

I shake my head, suddenly uneasy that I'm about to meet his mother. I mean, what if she hates me? Or says that I'm no good for his image or his career.

"Don't worry, she's gonna love you." I look over at him, wondering how he knew what I was thinking. "When you get nervous, you start to pick at the ends of your hair. I know you're not looking for anything in there, so it's just nerves. Don't worry, babe, we all have them. Before a game I get all clammy 'til I'm in my zone."

"Thank you for saying that."

"Of course. Now come over and give me those lips,

I've been staring at them for hours."

"How about I give them to you here?" I ask, sliding my hand inside of his shorts.

"Not before you meet my mom."

"I have gum," I offer, pulling his slacked cock out of the soft fabric of his shorts. He hardens in my hold, arching his hips towards my mouth. Without another word, I take full control of him, twirling my tongue over the head and then licking his shaft before going down on him. He moans the moment my lips seal fully around his head and take him deep.

I feel the car turn onto what seems like a dirt road, then stop. He weaves his fingers into my hair and I want to make sure that we haven't arrived. "Don't stop; I only pulled over, baby."

I whimper, sucking him. He holds my hair in a messy mound on the top of my head. *He tastes delicious.* So perfect and sweet, and smells like Bain. I let go of him with my hand and brace my weight above him to ensure that I have a good angle as I suck him like a maniac.

"Yes, babe. Make me come in your—" His sentence is cut off by his explosion and obscene cursing mixed with his animalistic grunts. Delicious cum drenches my throat. Immediately, I swallow it all down and suck him slowly, cleaning him 'til his cock is empty. Finally, on my way up, with my lips fiercely gripping him, I pull away and make a popping sound. I smile in satisfaction, staring into his light eyes as he holds my hair.

"That's where you had me, the first time I met you with those fucking lips."

"Are you saying you only like me for my sexual talents, Mr. Adams?"

"No, there's so much more to you than that. But your lips are something, Arion. Something else."

He readjusts himself and pulls back onto the main road. His phone rings on the drive and he answers it over the car's hands-free.

"Hey, Bain, are you guys almost here?" his dad asks.

"Yup, Arion had to pee so I pulled over for a minute, but we're back on the road."

"Good, we'll see you soon."

I stare at Bain with a scowl on my face. "I really do need to pee."

He glances at the water bottle between us and I pick it up, slapping him on the arm with it.

"Ouch, you know that's abuse, right?"

I just shake my head, happy to see him smile. For the last week, he's either sulked around about the news of Kinsey or been on the basketball court. I'm hoping getting him away from everything will keep him in a positive frame of mind.

"Fine," he grumbles, pulling up to a gas station. I slide my flip-flops on and strut inside.

After exiting the restroom, Bain is waiting for me. We hurry to the car and make the quick five-minute drive. The facility is nice. It's a huge ranch-style house with a ton of property surrounding it. As we walk inside, I take deep breaths, remembering what he said. *She's gonna love you.*

I hope he's right. We check in at the desk and get visitor's passes, then we head outside where I immediately see Bain's father, whom I recently met. He's standing next to Bain's mom and a smile beams across her face when she sees me. *That's a good sign.*

"Hey, Mom," Bain says, leaning down his large frame and hugging her. "How are you doing?"

"I'm better now. Thank you for coming."

"Of course. Mom, this is Arion. Arion, this is my mom, Renee."

"It's a pleasure to finally meet you," I say extending my hand to her.

"That's nonsense, dear. Give me a hug."

I embrace her, closing my eyes, feeling all of my anxiety wash away. *She likes me.* I think my fear of rejection comes from my childhood. Since I lost my parents at such a young age, I never felt like I really belonged anywhere or that anyone truly loved me. It's been so long since I've had parents like this to hug. I can barely remember how it felt to hold my grandma. I guess that's why I always gravitated towards Barb and Jeff. Speaking of…I need to call them, or just stop by for a visit.

"It's nice to meet you, Arion," she says.

"It's nice to meet you as well, Renee." She smiles and we all take our seats. There are lots of groups of other families all seated at the different tables. Bain said today was a standard visiting day; they get one per month. I couldn't imagine, but for their recovery, it's what's best. "How was the drive?" she asks us.

"It was good. Arion slept the whole way, so I got to think a lot about things."

"I'm going to run to the kitchen and get us some ice," Jack, Bain's dad, says.

"Bain, what do you know?" she asks. I know exactly what she's referring to – the news about Kinsey.

Bain gets nervous and swallows hard. I take my hand and rest it on his, to let him know that I'm right here. "Dad probably knows more. He talked to the FBI after the arrest."

"He's told me everything and it just doesn't make sense."

"It makes more sense now that someone did this to her, than the BS that cop was feeding us since the beginning. I knew she didn't do it. She wouldn't have."

"I know, baby, and I'm sorry I didn't believe you before. I was so lost and such a mess. I can barely remember those times; it's all such a blur."

"That's a good thing. I wish I could forget it all myself."

"I'm sorry, Arion. I know this isn't what you want to hear the first time that we all meet," Renee says.

"It's okay. This is very important. I'm here to talk about anything that you all want to."

"She's right," Bain's father says, setting down four

cups of ice. "We should talk about your son, who's about to join the NBA, and which team's gonna draft him."

"I can't tell you how proud of you I am. I know Kinsey would be too."

"Thank you, guys."

"Is there anywhere that you want to go?"

Bain looks at me and smiles, enveloping his hand around mine and says, "Anywhere that this woman will follow me to, I'll go."

Holding his hand tightly, I replay his words in my mind.

CHAPTER 31

-Bain-

As nice as it was to see my mom and see how well she's doing, this is where I need to be, alone with my girl. Even if it's only for a few days, both of us need it tremendously. As I mix us both a drink and watch her through the windows of the beach house, I can tell she's relaxed and at peace. She's got her feet rested up on the large, round ottoman and is just watching the waves crash against the shore. As I walk outside, she turns and looks at me and I ask her, "You like the water, don't you?"

"I love it."

"So do I. Here," I say, passing her the drink and sitting next to her. I stretch my arm behind her and she gets comfy on my chest. Both of us stare out into the vast horizon. There aren't a lot of people in the water, but lots walk by enjoying the nice June day.

"Can we stay here forever?"

"You've said that before," I tease her. "You did in New York and now."

"It's been nice to get away."

"This might sound crazy, but just hear me out, okay?"

She kisses my neck and says, "Of course."

"Quit your job. Help me manage my career."

"Bain, that's crazy. Plus, you have James."

"And he's busy. Things are only going to get crazier."

"I don't know. You haven't even been signed with anyone yet."

"Are you doubting my abilities?" I joke.

"Absolutely not."

"Good," I respond and set my drink down, kissing her soft lips, then guiding her to lie down on the large outdoor couch. For being a woman that knows what she wants, she sure lets me take control when I need it. We are a good pair like that. There are times I need her to control me.

She takes her hands and knots them into the back of my hair. I weave mine tightly into the back of hers and take my time trailing my lips over her mouth, beginning slowly then gaining more access. Finally, with our tongues fully connected, I kiss her the way I love. Her knees are slacked and my dick is as hard as ever.

"God, I wanna fuck you so badly."

"Then do it."

"There are people a hundred yards away."

"So, let them watch. I want your cock inside of me now and I don't want to wait."

I stare at her, so taken aback by her words that it almost makes me come thinking about what she wants me to do. "Dammit, Bain, fuck me."

Placing my hand over her mouth, I tell her, "Shhh, be quiet."

She smirks at me, reaching between us and pulls her pants down. I slide my shorts down a little and look around. Then grip my cock at the base and slam into her. She cries out in pleasure, but my hand still covers those sweet lips, muffling the noise.

"You asked for it. Now be fucking quiet."

Her breathing is heavy. Her chest heaving up and down, up and down. But my demand quieted her noises. Taking both of my hands, I hold her face and fuck her gently. I'm so turned on that someone walking by could see us. Her pussy is my kingdom – it was made for my cock and I love how perfectly we fit together.

Working her like this, she pulls my neck to her mouth and begins to suck on my skin. It helps to muffle her uncontrollable noises so I let her, knowing that it might leave a mark. It's better than having to slow down.

"Fuck, baby, I love your pussy."

Saying the word "love" so freely makes me realize that maybe my feelings for her are more than I ever intended them to be. I do love more than her pussy. Fuck, I love every goddamn thing about her.

Her heels are dug into my legs, holding us tightly together. Then she relinquishes her orgasm over to me and I lose it. She tightens that sweet pussy, holding my dick like a vice, causing me to grunt like an animal. Letting go, I come inside of this beautiful woman I love. Dammit, I love her. She told me to not have feelings for her and to just fuck, but I've failed miserably.

How could I not, with what we've been through and helped each other cope with? I slow my movements, so torn up by my mind-fuck. She protests my stopping and grabs my ass, pushing and pulling me in and out of her.

Upon opening my eyes, all of my fears fade away. Her eyes are closed and her bottom lip is sucked into her mouth. I keep my movements strong, and watch her as her face changes. Pleasure takes over her body, blood pulsing under her light skin, which is now covered in a sheen of sweat. Staring at her, she never opens her eyes and only trembles lightly. However, it lasts for at least a full minute and I don't stop as aftershocks give little jolts here and there. I don't know how to handle this or why I didn't see it coming. Maybe I should talk to her this weekend and be honest and tell her my feelings?

"I swear to God, Bain, if you put me in that water, I'll—"

"What?" I ask holding Arion in my arms, pretending to throw her into the freezing Atlantic.

"I'll leave, that's what."

"Oh, are you going to drive away in your invisible car?" I tease.

She glares at me and I tense up, pretending to toss her. Instead I sit down with her resting comfortably in my hold.

"I would never do anything you didn't want me to, even joking," I reassure her.

"Thank you. Not only for that, but this entire weekend. It's been great so far."

"It has, hasn't it?"

She nods her head and yawns a little. I watch her feet as she moves her toes in the sand. "Do you want to go out for dinner tonight?" I ask.

"Yeah, that would be great."

"So, I know we said no cell phones this weekend, but James left me a message. The Knicks want me to come work out at their facility. It would be close to home if I got drafted there."

"That's really good, right?"

"For sure. When a team wants you, this is what you hope for."

"What all will you do when you're there?"

"I'll practice, meet everyone, do interviews, and see if overall I'd be a good fit. I'd love to go to the Knicks."

"When are you going?"

"Tuesday. Will you come with me?

"I have work."

"If you'd quit, you could come and not have to worry about a thing."

"I can't do that, Bain."

"Come on, babe, please." I give her my best guilt trip. Being away from her makes me sick. I can't imagine doing it all the time.

"Wherever you get drafted, we'll figure things out. But I'm not quitting my job."

I kiss her hair, not pushing the subject any further. I can't push things with her. I already tried last night to tell her how I was feeling. She instantly clammed up and shut me down, looking at me like she did in the beginning when she kept reiterating the rules. I don't need that anymore. I've accepted our relationship for what it is. I just want her and I'll take her any way that I can get her. End of story.

"Come on then, let's get ready for dinner."

While Arion is in the shower, I check my phone. Thankfully, James hasn't called again. Compared to his messages earlier, this is nice. I told him I was taking a few days and he now seems to respect that.

I get dressed in a pair of faded jeans and a t-shirt. I don't care that my tattoos are showing tonight. In fact we're going somewhere that accepts them. Heading back into the master bedroom, Arion enters and my dick gets hard. She's in jeans like me, with a thin white tank top and clearly no bra. Her frozen nipples are hard and erect, pushing against the fabric. Looking down at myself in my jeans and white t-shirt, we are so much alike.

"Come on, we don't wanna be late," I respond.

She smirks at me and walks by, sliding on her flip-flops.

"So where are we going?" she asks, buckling her seat belt.

"Dinner."

"No shit. Where?"

"I can't tell you that. What I can tell you is there is more to the night than just the meal."

She contemplates my words, thinking really hard about them. I love watching her wheels spin. She looks absolutely adorable when she's deep in thought.

Checking my phone, I look at the directions one more time and pull onto the freeway. God, I hope she doesn't freak out and likes what I have in store for tonight. She has talked about it before, so it's not like what I have planned will be totally out of left field. If she doesn't want to do it, then she doesn't have to. But I sure as hell am. Fuck, I can't wait.

Glancing at Arion, she looks relaxed. "Does Virginia have a basketball team?" she asks.

I shake my head. "No, unfortunately they don't. You like it here?"

"Yeah. It's relaxing, maybe it's more the water than anything."

"You wanna live on the water?"

"I would love to."

"Then we'll live on the water," I confirm.

"Bain, come on, you know that might not happen. What if you got picked by Denver or somewhere without the ocean?"

"Then we could live on a lake. Fuck, A, I'd buy you a lake."

"You really are something else."

"And so are you. So what's your choice? Wendy's or Taco Bell?"

She stares up at the two restaurants as they sit opposite each other in the parking lot. "Are you serious right now?"

"As serious as I've ever been. Come on, I told you I don't want to be late."

"To what, dinner?"

"No, what's after dinner."

"Fine. Wendy's. But whatever you have up your sleeve, it better be good."

"It will be, trust me."

I go through the drive through and order our food. She just stares at me. I'm not sure if she's pissed that we went through the drive through or if it's the fact that we are at Wendy's in general.

"We could've gone to Taco Bell if you'd prefer," I say with a mouthful of food. I haven't been eating like this lately and it tastes absolutely fucking delicious.

"I told you I'm fine. Stop worrying."

"Okay."

Once we finish our food, we make the short trip across the street, to where our appointment is. When I put the car in park, her jaw drops.

"Why are we here?" she asks.

"'Cause we have an appointment. Let's go!"

CHAPTER 32

-Arion-

Staring into the window of the crowded tattoo shop, I suddenly become uneasy. I know I told Bain that I wanted a tattoo, but I didn't think he would actually make it happen.

"Come on, babe, this guy is world renowned for his work. He used to work in Jersey and he's done a ton of mine, you're gonna love him, I promise."

"I don't know, Bain, I haven't even had the time to really think about it."

"It's okay. If you're not feeling it, you don't have to. I'm going to get Kinsey's portrait tattooed on my chest, so you'll have lots of time to think about yours."

He gives me a reassuring squeeze on the knee and we hop out of his car. The shop is in a strip mall. It all looks brand new and is very modern with all kinds of cool art all over. There are patrons inside and out, and the moment we walk in, Bain is recognized. "What up, man?" the guy behind the counter greets Bain, coming around to give him a hand shake.

"Not much, how's the new shop?" Bain asks.

"It's great, we're really busy."

Then another guy comes from the back. "I was just setting up for you guys. It's great to see you, bro."

"You too," Bain responds, shaking his hand. "Tommy, this is my…this is Arion."

He corrects himself and doesn't call me his girlfriend. I'm a tiny bit hurt by this. Then again, I have been the one who's been shut down and reserved when it comes to feelings. Plus I was very clear in the beginning, no feelings whatsoever. I told him we could try and see where things led, but that was it. There wasn't any more that I gave him to work with so I can understand what he's trying to do.

"It's great to meet you, Arion. Bain said this is your first tattoo?"

"Yeah, it is, so please forgive me if I'm a little nervous."

"It's all good. You can watch how Bain takes it. Come on back."

We head back to where Tommy has everything set up and he holds up a sketch. I can tell right way that the picture is of Kinsey.

"I love it," Bain exclaims.

"Good, now you know the drill."

Bain smirks at him, lifting his white t-shirt above his head. Once he has it off, he passes it to me and I set it in my lap, taking my seat next to Bain. I watch as Tommy shaves what little hair is on his chest, then the two guys talk about where to place the stencil.

Watching all this take place makes me think…do I really want to get a tattoo? And if I do, should it be something for Nate? I'm not sure how Bain would feel about that. Then again, he did bring me here after we talked about getting something together for each of us losing those closest to us.

Once the stencil is set, Bain checks it in the mirror, then lays back and looks at me as Tommy starts the first line of what I'm sure will be many.

"You okay?" he asks me.

"Yeah."

"What are you going to get?"

I shrug my shoulders unsure. The buzz of the tattoo gun is quieter than I expected. I watch Tommy do his work, keeping a steady line and think about what in the world I want to get.

"You're going to get something for Nate, right?" Bain asks.

I think about his question wondering how in the world he can be so cool with me getting a tattoo representing another guy. Granted, I know it's because I lost Nate, a lot like he lost his sister, and we've connected over that. It's a bond that has made us strong and that's brought us together.

"I really don't know, Bain. I'm torn."

"What are your thoughts?" he asks as if Tommy isn't

carving a needle into his chest. He's so calm and relaxed. It's almost like he likes the pain. I shake my head unable to give him a solid answer. "When you said you wanted to get a tattoo, what were you thinking?"

"I was thinking 'Nate' in cursive, but not now."

"Why?" he asks dead serious.

I look him straight in the eyes. "Because of you."

"That's why I brought you here. Get what your heart feels. If it's his name then get it."

I hear what he is saying, but I don't believe him. I don't believe that he would want to kiss every inch of my body including the part that said 'Nate.' Jesus, I finally have the opportunity to get a tattoo, but I can't decide.

"There are some books on the counter. If you wanna look through them, you can," Tommy offers.

"I want something different."

"I get that," Bain says. "What about a quote?"

The moment he says the word, I know what to get. "Learn from yesterday, live for today, hope for tomorrow."

"Albert Einstein?" Bain confirms.

I nod my head and he winks at me. "I love it, babe. Can I add it below mine too?"

"Sure."

I sit back feeling content, knowing what and where my tattoo will go. I've always envisioned one on my ribs, so that's an easy choice.

"Are you nervous?" Bain asks me.

"Not at all. More excited than anything."

"Let me wash it for you, baby."

I shake my head, still not sure how I made it through the hour tattoo. It was the worst pain I've ever endured. I can't even imagine touching my skin right now as it is finally not screaming at me. "Don't act like this. You have to wash it, so it's either you or me."

I scowl at Bain as he sits next to me. He's shirtless with the bandage still covering his chest. His tattoo of Kinsey is gorgeous. Tommy does amazing work; no wonder Bain has had him do so much of his.

Finally, he stands up and stares down at me with irritation in his eyes. "Either get up, or I'll pick you up and I'm sure it will hurt."

I know he's not joking so I stand on my own and take his hand as he extends it to me. Without speaking a word, he walks us to the bathroom and starts the shower. "Arms up," he orders coming over to me.

I listen, standing with my eyes fixated on his beautiful face. Reaching down, he gently grasps the hem of my shirt and kisses me before lifting it over my head. His lips still give me a stomach full of butterflies.

Next he moves to my pants and I let him take care of me. Taking control of us and the situation the way he has so many times. As I stand naked before him, he kneels in front of me. Steam from the shower begins to fill the room, warming my body, causing me to shiver. Placing a large warm hand on my abdomen, he grabs the corner of the tape that holds the bandage to my skin. "Ready?"

"Mm-hmm."

"God, you're beautiful," he says slowly peeling the tape off. I watch his tattooed hand, slow and steady. His patience and care makes any ounce of pain, vanish. Finally, he drops the ink-blood-stained bandage and stands, checking the water before shooing me in. I'm hesitant to get in without him, but he doesn't waste a second shredding off the rest of clothes and then tearing his bandage off, as well. He showed much more care and patience with me than himself. "Are you okay?" he asks, grabbing a bottle of soap off of the counter then sliding in next to me.

"I am. Thank you, Bain. Thank you for everything."

"Of course. Why don't you wash mine so you can see what it feels like. You don't need to use a lot of pressure, okay?"

I smirk at him and give my hand to him. He pumps a squirt of soap in it and says, "Wash your hands first."

I listen and then reach out for more soap. He gives it to me and I rub a lather together before pressing it against his hard chest. He doesn't look at what I'm doing, he only watches my eyes. I make small circular motions over the beautiful portrait of Kinsey. When the tattoo was finished and Bain's chest was compared to the actual picture, they were identical.

"That's enough," he says and turns into the water, the soap rinsing away leaving a masterpiece. Below it is our matching quote, which I absolutely love. Holding out the soap, he squirts some on his fingers and goes to touch my tattoo. I freeze waiting for his fingers to make contact with my skin. "Are you okay if I do this?"

I nod my head and he holds my hip with one hand and takes the other, leaving gentle strokes, soothing my angry skin. "This looks so fucking hot on you."

I can't help the smile that covers my face. "Rinse now," he commands.

I rinse and turn the water off. Both of us are so hot for one another that you could cut the tension in the air with a knife. I know what I want. I want Bain and his cock to do what he does best and I want it now. Watching him move the white towel over his body almost makes me tear it away. I get bits and pieces of Mr. Sexy Man as he dries himself. Sex. Sin. Cock. Tattoos. Then just when I can't take anymore, he drops it.

"Don't look at me like that," I warn. His eyes are hooded and his stance shows he's about to take me at any moment. "Better run, then."

I lick my bottom lip and bolt out of the bathroom, stark naked. The cool breeze on my skin chills me, not to mention how it makes the skin of my tattoo tingle. Bain is right behind me, his presence this close is not something that can go unnoticed. I don't make it far, weaving in and out of this elegant home, before he catches me by one of my wrists.

I spin in his hold and he turns me back towards him.

"Gotcha, beautiful."

I laugh and give in to him, the same way I always do.

"Maybe I wanted you to."

"We'll have to see about that," he says scooping me up in his arms and taking me into the bedroom. He uses extra caution, holding me to make sure that his hand doesn't touch my tattoo nor does he move in a way that will irritate it. Gently, he lays me on the bed and says, "Stay there." I listen, sitting up and watching him walk back into the bathroom. He comes out with a bottle of Aquaphor and squirts a dab on his finger then straddles my legs with his and begins to very gently apply a thin coat.

"You gotta keep it moist, but don't suffocate it, okay?"

"I think you better keep it moist," I respond reaching down and grabbing his cock. Holding it tightly in my grip, he shakes his head and puts some ointment on his tattoo. Then as he wipes his hands, his hips begin to move in my hold, pushing in and out. "You want me to cum on you?"

"Maybe."

"We'll see," he says pulling my hand away and pinning it against the mattress, then he crashes inside of me. My pussy is instantly consumed with all of him. I love the feeling, so full and hard. Now with both of my hands pinned out to my side, Bain looks at me, his hard dick inside of me, and says, "Jesus Christ, babe, this pussy of yours is amazing."

I tighten my muscles, holding fiercely onto him, as he loves the inside of my body. Then I tighten myself around him and immediately want to come. The pleasure is too great, causing me to let up. Bain grunts above me, both of my knees are slacked to the side and my hands are held under his, leaving me fully in his control.

I can't stop the cries of passion, what he's doing to me is too much to handle. These slow, long thrusts are pushing me over the edge. Then Bain says, "My kingdom, your pussy is my kingdom," and I lose all logic and fall under his spell. My body quavers and writhes on its own, with my eyes tightly shut, enjoying this bliss. Then Bain lets his release go, his noises are the loudest they've ever been, causing me to focus on him in this moment. The veins on his neck change and his tattoos morph as his muscles strain from underneath. The pressure from his hold on my wrists is so tight that it ignites something inside of me. Something deep within, a craving I've been searching for since the day...I lost him.

CHAPTER 33

-Bain-

Being with Arion makes everything right. Everything is so different than it was before. Finally, I have a glimpse of how good things can be, that my life still has potential, and now I have to say goodbye to her. I'm not sure how to accomplish something so overpowering, but James has set up workouts for me with three NBA teams. I know it's only for a week, but saying goodbye like this feels like what could happen if I get drafted somewhere she doesn't want to go.

We haven't even spoken of our feelings, so for all I know, what I'm feeling is totally different than what she is. Maybe she needs a break and some time. I know for me, I can't get enough of her. Not having her with me sort of scares me. I gave up pills, stopped obsessing over Kinsey's case, and let myself fall down a hole with Arion. She has been my curative, taking away everything bad that was hurting me before.

"There you are," she says, coming out front and catching me off guard. It's far too early to be awake, but my mind told me otherwise.

"Good morning, baby," I say, opening my arms to her. She comes over in nothing but one of my t-shirts and crawls onto my lap.

"Morning. Are you okay?"

"I am now," I respond, too afraid to tell her about my three-city stop. It was one thing when I was training locally, somewhere that was within a drive. Now, I have to fly to Phoenix and Memphis. If one of those teams wants me, they are sure to fly me back and extend things even longer.

"What do you want to do today?"

"This," she says holding me a little closer and exhaling longingly.

"I can do this all day, baby."

Lifting her head with that sexy ass smirk written all over her perfect face, she stares at me. "Are you for real?"

"I think so," I respond, taking her head in my hands and directing her ear to my chest. She presses it firmly against my shirt and listens. "This is real, what you do to me is real. I know you said no feelings, but Arion, call me crazy if I'm the only one feeling this."

She doesn't move and I pray that the words I want to hear come out of her mouth. That she says something and doesn't let me sit here like a fucking loser spilling my heart out.

"You need to know this. I can't keep hiding these

feelings any longer, especially since I'm leaving town soon."

Finally she moves and looks at me. "You're just going to New York."

"As well as Phoenix and Memphis. James emailed me with the news, both the Suns and the Grizzlies want me to come work out for them and I want you to come with me. I *need* you to come with me."

She lies back down without another word. Taking my hand, I run my fingers through her messy blonde hair. *Dammit, I should have stayed fucking quiet. She's clamming up on me.*

"Come on, A, say something."

"I don't know what to say."

"Quit your job and come with me."

Tears fill her eyes and she says, "Don't start with that again. I can't. I have a job that I love and you know that."

"Don't you think you could love working for me? I'm sure James needs the help. I'm going to get a huge deal, so I can pay you double what you make now."

"Bain, it's not about the money, plus I don't know the first thing about the NBA."

"Come on, babe. Just give it a chance."

"Bain, I can't just drop everything. We don't even know where you'll get drafted. Besides, I do have commitments in New Jersey that I can't just walk away from."

"I'm not asking you to walk away from anything."

"But you are. You're asking me to leave my job," she snaps and climbs off of my lap, her ass hanging out of that shirt, and I instantly regret opening my mouth. I should have just left without her and dealt with my own insecurities.

Rage consumes me, almost more for my own stupidity than anything else. I did this. Then I remember my mom always telling me when I fucked up, *Make it right, Bain. It's not too late, it's never too late.*

Bolting out of the chair, I go inside. Arion is nowhere on the main level. Sprinting upstairs, I find her dressed and tossing her clothes into her suitcase. "No, baby. Come on, let's talk about this. You're blowing things way out of proportion."

"Am I? I think I heard you pretty clearly. I've told you again and again that I'm not going to leave my job, but you won't drop it. I can't turn over my life to you like I did with Nate. You know how that ended and I won't put myself in that situation again."

Stepping in front of her, she stares at me like the strong woman that she is. I rub my thumb over her plump lips, holding her chin. "Don't you see what you mean to me? Please don't take that away."

Staring down at her, my heart is erratic. She's about to leave and give up on what we have, all because I can't be away from her. It hasn't been long, but goddammit she means the fucking world to me. She doesn't answer me, so I take her hand and place it over my heart and then rest mine on hers trying to feel the rhythm. Tears wash out the corners of her eyes and she pulls away from me.

"Please take me home, Bain."

Stepping to her again, I say, "You are home. Anywhere I am is your home. Don't you fucking get it?!"

"Don't yell at me."

"You're going to throw this all away because you're scared. I'm not him, A. I'm not going anywhere or getting deployed. I'm sorry I don't want to be away from you."

"Bain, don't fucking go down that road."

"Arion, please. Don't you see how fucked up we used to be? Don't make things go back to the way they were."

"You did this. You're not going to control me. Things were fine how they were. Now you're trying to change everything."

"Do you think I can control this? Because if you do, then you're dead wrong."

"I don't fucking know what to think, but I wanna go home. Now!"

Nodding my head repeatedly, I finally back down. She doesn't give a shit about how I feel. She's obviously too tortured and burdened by the past, just like I was. She's pulled me out of it; I just need to figure out some way to pull her from this darkness too. I need to make her see the light. Right now, there's nothing I can do. She won't listen and wants to leave. Maybe if we get on the road, she'll hear me out when we are trapped in the car for five hours.

"Yeah, James, I fucking heard you."

"Jesus, are you all right?"

"I already told you once, I'm fine. If you could please just stick to emailing me like I asked, you wouldn't have to deal with my bullshit."

"This is the last call for all passengers boarding flight 238 to Phoenix."

"That's me, I gotta run. I'll email you later."

I hang up with James, feeling a bit regretful for how I went off on him. But Christ, the man is worse than an overbearing mom and my nerves are shot. It's been four days since my fight with Arion and I haven't heard a word from her. She refused to see my side of things on the drive home, and right now I can't change what happened. As much as I just want to be with her, I can't. One of the worst parts is that my career has me here and I have to take that seriously. Checking my messages, she still hasn't responded.

I guess I blew it by opening my mouth. Did I really think she would up and quit and just chase me around the US? That's fucking insane to ask someone to do that anyways. For the last few days, our fight has been all that's replayed in my mind. Walking down the tarmac, I prepare to board the plane and feel sick that I'm going so far away without her. Fuck, I wish I had some pills to numb the pain. Inside, I'm such a mess. There are so many thoughts that swirl around, from Kinsey, to that piece of shit detective, and then my beautiful Arion. Maybe I'll be able to sleep on the plane, God knows I need to. As I get situated in the front row, I'm thankful to James for booking this; he not only got me the front row, but the seat next to me. Pulling my hat down low, I pop my hood up and sink back against the plush leather, stretching my legs out in front of me.

Visions of Arion invade all of my senses. From the first night in the alley to fucking her on my kitchen counter, it all consumes me. Before her, I was hell-bent on Kinsey's case, and now, none of that matters like it used to. I guess I shouldn't have become dependent on her. That's where the feelings started. She warned me not to do it, but I did. She helped me deal with all of the pain I was experiencing. Then I broke her rules.

CHAPTER 34

-*Arion*-

Do not text him back. Do not text him back. Do not text him back. Lying face down on my bed, I know I can't text him. But he's relentless and won't give up. Rolling over, I stare up at the white ceiling replaying the events that took place a few days back. Since the moment Bain dropped me off, I instantly regretted everything. Being away from him has hit me hard, but inside I know it's best to protect my heart. The pain I'm feeling now is nothing compared to what I experienced when I lost Nate. It was utterly debilitating – crippling. It took me over a month just to get out of bed. At least this time I've managed to go in to work. Maybe I've been a little late, but I've been there.

I try to close my eyes again, but Bain's words are loud and clear. *Quit your job and come work for me.* He knows me so well, and it still baffles me how he thought I would give up everything I've worked so hard for.

Getting out of bed, I pad across the room and peer into the living room. Aubrey is still not home, so I grab a bottle of water before heading back to bed. My phone rings and I'm reluctant to answer it, but I catch a glimpse of the screen and notice it's Barb.

"Hey," I say in a quiet tone.

"Hi, honey, how are you?"

"I'm okay."

"What's wrong?"

"Just got a lot going on in my head."

"Don't we all? Do you want to talk about anything?"

"No, that's okay. It's just nice to hear your voice, you always make things better."

"Thanks, dear. I was calling because I got the results from Zeus' blood work and everything is normal."

"Oh, good. Thank you for taking him."

"Of course. Are you sure you don't want to talk?"

"I'm sure. I have to get to work soon and I didn't sleep well, that's all, so I'm going to take a nap. But I'll try and stop by tomorrow to see my baby boy."

"Okay. Keep your head up, sweetheart."

"Thanks," I respond and hang up. I know I have about an hour before I have to be at work and I don't want to be late again. It's become quite a habit for me these last few days. Speaking of habits, I spark a cigarette and inhale deeply. Knowing Bain would be pissed if he knew I was smoking again, but it doesn't stop me. I need something to calm myself down.

Lying here, all of our time plays in my mind. From the moment I caught sight of him laughing at my brazenness at the bar, to the alley, then everything spiraling afterwards. I fought any feelings that were possibly creeping in by reminding myself that this was only about sex. It always had been, but deep inside, I know it was more.

Fuck. Taking another drag I finally put the cigarette out and roll over. Sleep, sleep, sleep is the only thing that can take this away. Just a few minutes and then I'll get my ass in the shower…

"Fine, Bain, you want me to tell you the truth? I'm scared, fucking terrified, that what we have is all going to come crashing down."

"No, baby, how could you even think that? I won't let it."

"How can you promise that? You just got drafted then traded to the fucking Clippers. That's LA, it's a whole other world out there and across the country."

"Listen to me," he pleads getting down at my level and kneeling in front of the chair. *"It's not that different from New York."*

"I just don't understand why you couldn't have gone to the Knicks or the Nets, or even the 76ers. I mean, somewhere East Coast."

"Does it matter? We'll be together and to me that's what's important."

I rest my face in my hands, so frustrated that we are still in this situation. I know I should jump at this, but something is telling me no. I just don't know what it is.

"Please, baby, just let me take care of you."

"Bain, I can't sit back and depend on you like that."

"Please, just say yes. Marry me and make me the happiest man

alive, I promise I'll never, ever, let you down..."

I wake sweaty and out of it. Blinking a few times, it takes me a moment to realize that it was all just a dream. Thank God it was only a dream! I hear Aubrey come in the front door. Finally. I've barely seen her for the past four days. She comes straight into my room and sits on my bed.

"Hey, I thought you had work today."

I check my phone and realize that I overslept. *Dammit.* Sitting up, I bolt out of my bed and into the closet, dressing as fast as I can. "I do have to work and I was supposed to be there over an hour ago."

"Jesus, A, are you serious? Haven't you been late every day since this whole Bain situation?"

"Don't even start with that shit, Aubrey."

She's watching me, trying to understand where my sudden outburst came from.

"I'm sorry, I just don't need any shit right now."

"I'm not here to give you any shit. I was going to recommend that you call him."

"Yeah, that's not going to happen."

"I just hate seeing you like this."

"Yeah, well, I fucking hate feeling like this, but it's for the best. It couldn't have lasted forever."

Leaning down, I give her a hug and run out of the apartment, heading to work as fast as I can. I can't believe I overslept. I was late the other day and Gavina, my district manager, called the store after my shift started, asking for me. Of course, I wasn't there and she was pissed.

Just as I pull up, Bain calls me – again. I hit decline. I can't deal with him right now. Then the moment I walk in, I know I'm fucked. This time instead of a missed phone call, Gavina is inside and not only observing the store and talking to the employees and customers, she's behind the counter making drinks. I put my head down and hang my shit up, then pull on my apron and prepare to face the music.

The moment Gavina sees me, she shakes her head and points at the office. *Sonofabitch.* Being reprimanded like a toddler, I walk in and pray that it's just another ass chewing like she's given me before.

She comes in with anger in her eyes, and I say, "I'm so sorry that I was—"

She cuts me off, raising her hand and slams the door. "Arion, save it. Do you have any idea how much I've stuck my neck out on the line for you to manage this store?"

I nod my head as she continues. "Well, you've sure pissed on me, like you don't give a shit about this job."

"I'm so sorry, it won't happen again."

"You're right, it won't. Because this time you've left me no choice. My boss came through the drive through this morning and you had no supervisor on duty."

"But—" I try and cut her off to explain, but she just continues.

"If you could imagine how disappointed he was when your team members said there was no manager here. You know the rules. You have to have a manager on at all times, whether it's you or your assistant manager. I tried to call you, Arion, and you didn't answer. You've shown disregard for this store and your team lately. Your shift started over an hour ago and I don't know what's going on with you, but I can't have it going on here. You need to handle your personal business and I need you to turn in your keys."

"Gavina, please. It—"

"Don't waste your breath. Either turn in your keys or I'll have the building rekeyed."

I stare back at her stunned. *She just fired me.* Reaching into my pocket, I toss my keys and badge on the desk. Then I turn around to leave. Knowing Gavina well, there is no point in arguing with her or trying to make my point. I made my bed, now I have to lie in it. As I walk out, I slowly pull my apron over my head and grab my stuff. Glancing back at my employees, they are all staring at me. I can't bear to look at them or even wave. I get in my car, immediately dreading going home. God, I wish Bain was here.

I'm not sure if I can crawl back into that fucking bed again. I feel like I've spent all my time in it lately. Driving home, I'm in shock. I should be crying or upset, I just lost my fucking job. A job that I absolutely loved. But I'm not. The only thing that I feel is numbness. Grabbing my phone, I go to call Bain, I have to. He'll know what to say and how to help me. *What am I thinking?* I no longer have that option. God, I've really ruined everything in my life.

There's no way I'm that dependent on him. Or am I? My mind is swirling with a million different scenarios. I got fired, when all along Bain wanted me to quit. I go to call him automatically, when I know I can't. Jesus, maybe I can't push him away as easily as I thought. Although part of me wants to...I'm not sure it's possible.

CHAPTER 35

-Bain-

Whatever happens, please don't let me get drafted to Phoenix. Pulling onto the freeway, it's hot as fuck, the organization's weird, and it's the last place I can see myself living. Getting in my rental car, I make the quick drive to the hotel and can't wait to relax. My body is beyond sore. I think working out for these two teams has been an eye opener for me. I don't know how I'll make it through Memphis, but I guess I'll find out tomorrow.

I really shouldn't be complaining though; it's all a way to keep my mind busy. A way to focus on things other than the reality that I pissed her off and she left me. Again, I call her. It actually rings. She's not declining my calls, but she's still not answering.

Hanging up. I check my messages. James, James, James, my dad, and James again. The one from my dad alarms me and I have to listen to it again.

"Bain, I hate to tell you this while you're focusing on your workouts, but Anthony pleaded not guilty, this whole thing is going to trial. The prosecutor called me today and said she wants all three of us to testify. Just call me, okay, son?"

I delete his message right away. Fuck that motherfucker, not guilty. The guy fucking took her life; he robbed her from so much. How can he plead not guilty? For the rest of the drive I listen to James' messages then head straight for my room. Once I'm inside, I call room service for my dinner and boot up my laptop, preparing an email response to James' messages, like I have been lately. If I keep busy with this shit, it will keep my mind off of the nagging fact that I don't have Arion and that asshole plead not guilty.

Sitting back, I type away. Then it happens and my heart stops. My whole world comes to a stop as her ring tone comes on my phone. Without even looking at the screen I answer. "Baby?"

She doesn't respond and I listen for any hint that she's there. "Arion, are you there?"

I hear her voice. It's far away, but it's there. I can tell she's talking to someone. Waiting, I listen trying to make out what she is saying. Anything at all would help me right now, then she mumbles and the phone sounds muffled. "Arion, please talk to me."

Finally she does, her voice is timid, almost broken, but it's her. "Hey."

"Hi," I respond. She's still silent and I ask, "How are you?"

"I've been better."

"I know, baby, me too."

There's an awkward silence between us and I say, "I miss you so much."

Exhaling loudly into the phone, she says, "Listen, Bain, I have a lot going on right now, I don't think I can do this."

"Then talk to me, baby, let me help you."

"I can't. I'm sorry, I just can't."

The line goes silent before I can say anything else. I wonder if she actually meant to call me, as there was truly no point to that conversation. Leaning back in the chair, I exhale and stare at the celling. How did I lose the girl who stole my heart? I need to figure out how to get her back.

"It's nice to meet you," I say, shaking hands with the assistant coach of the Grizzlies.

"You too. We can't thank you enough for coming here."

"Of course. Thank you for having me."

"How was your flight?" he asks and I follow him into the huge gym where there are a few guys practicing.

"It was nice. I came in from Phoenix, so it was nice to leave the heat." After Jim gives me a rundown of the facility, one of the ball guys from the middle of the court passes me the ball. The moment I have it in my hands, I shoot it. I know I'm pretty far behind the three-point line but my range is deep, and draining this in front of all these people would be sweet. As the ball floats through the air, everyone in the room turns and watches it. *Bam, nothing but net, baby.*

I smirk, thankful that although I'm a mess inside, my game isn't affected. Over the next hour, I can't tell you how many balls I sink. I'm definitely in the zone. Then we move on to defense. It's not my best area, but I've been working on it the last few years and it's improved. Lastly, I get to scrimmage, before meeting with the coaches and the staff.

Quickly, I dry off after my shower and get dressed before sitting down with everyone. Although I never imagined it…I could actually see myself playing here. I know Arion won't be part of that dream anymore. She's made that clear and since she's ignoring me, my gut is telling me to push forward and not look back. I've thought about it a lot and wish I knew of a way to make things work with her, but her pain runs very deep and she's stubborn beyond reason.

Leaving the locker room, I walk down the long, white hall 'til I reach the office where we are meeting. Knocking once, I head inside.

"Mr. Adams," their head coach says, welcoming me.

"It's great to meet you in person, sir." I shake his and then everyone else's hand. We all sit down. I'm directly across from the head coach, the assistant coach is next to him, and then the general manager.

"You were quite impressive on the court today."

"Thank you, sir. Your facility is great."

"We would love to have you on our team, but you're projected to be drafted pretty high in the first round. We don't have a pick 'til the thirteenth spot. If you could imagine our dilemma, in order to make this work we're going to have to figure out some sort of deal. So tell us, why are you the guy to go with?"

I'm a little unsure how to answer the question, so I follow my gut.

"I can't promise you guys anything. Trust me, if I could, then I would. I've learned that recently. But what I can tell you is if you pick me, I'll work my ass off, day in and day out to help you win. I know my skills and they are only going to get better with your coaching staff and the competition. I was born to play this game."

"Mr. Adams?" the assistant coach asks me.

"Please call me Bain."

"Bain, I have to be frank with you. It concerns me that you didn't finish playing your senior year. I've heard what happened to your sister, and I'm sorry. But with that, there are quite a few mixed rumors that I'm not sure I want on this team."

"Thank you and believe me, I respect that. However, I had to make a choice this year. I lost a very important person in my life and was in no shape to be on the court. I knew if I was to force my playing, it would hurt me more than taking a step back, my parents needed me at home so that's what I needed to do. I knew there was a chance of it jeopardizing my chances in the draft, but ultimately my family is number one. With the time off, I did a lot of soul searching and now know that I was born to play ball. I need it, plain and simple."

The three men look at each other and nod their heads. "Well, that was just the answer we were looking for, son. Can we convince you to stay the rest of the week and show you around our beautiful city?"

"I'm flying back tonight, but talk to my manager. I'm not sure what he has booked for me, if it can work, I'd love too."

"You're a bright young man, Bain," the head coach says and then continues, "I was hesitant in bringing you here, but after speaking with you and seeing you play, I'm going to do everything I can to make Memphis your home."

"Thank you all for having me. I'm looking forward to that possibility."

We exchange our goodbyes and I leave. Calling Arion the moment I'm outside, I need to talk to her. I can't have this burden any longer. My life is moving fast and I *want* her by my side – I *need* her by my side.

CHAPTER 36

-Arion-

I think I've flipped through the channels on the TV about a gazillion times. Aubrey, God love her, ran to get us some dinner while I sulk in my jobless and Bainless existence. I know I should talk to him and work past things. But I can't. I just can't. I fucking can't. Yes, something is seriously fucking wrong with me and I know it.

Finally, I land on the news. It's the only thing that seems somewhat interesting. It's sad, but dammit, so am I. Rolling to my side, I seem to study the news anchor more than what he is saying and notice how he resembles Bain. They are both tall, have short brown hair, and I bet this guy has tattoos hidden underneath his suit.

Aubrey comes through the door, taking my mind off the news. She lifts the pizza box and smiles at me. "I got your favorite."

"Thanks, babe," I say turning the TV down.

"Of course." She sets it down and grabs two beers from the refrigerator and some paper towels. "Did you miss me?" she asks jokingly.

I nod my head; she always makes things better, so much better. I haven't eaten much, lately and finally feel like I can stomach something, thank God. She sits down and we each grab a slice, watching the news. That's one of the things about Aubrey, she doesn't pry or make me get deep with things, she lets me just be.

"Holy shit, did you hear about this, A?" she asks as the news anchor starts to talk about a prisoner of war. "I meant to tell you yesterday, it's been all over the news."

"In news across the US, thirty-one-year-old Darren Spars finally returned home to his quiet town of Kittredge, Colorado after being held captive for almost a year. Spars was missing and presumed dead, before bravely escaping from captivity in Afghanistan. Authorities aren't saying much about how or why he was taken. Darren has since asked for privacy, while he readjusts to life at home with his wife and three children. In other news…" The reporter trails off into another story and I can't believe how lucky that man is.

"Pretty crazy, huh?"

I can't answer her as I'm lost in my own crazy thoughts. My mind immediately goes to Nate. God, I wish that could've been him. *But it can't and never will be.* They found enough DNA evidence among human remains from his last mission site to change his status from "missing in action" to "killed in action." I just have to accept the truth and move forward, but it's hard not to want to wish the truth away.

Accepting that Nate is gone forever solidifies my feelings for Bain. As much as I want to fight them...I can't. Not anymore. He's so good to me and I really could see a future with him. I've sat here miserable for almost a week acting like I don't care, fighting the roller coaster of emotions that are going through me. When really, it all boils down to one simple fact. I'm fucking in love with him. Looking down at my uneaten pizza and sunken in stomach, I know I'm really empty without him.

When we are together, we both thrive. We can live and we can breathe. I don't want a fairy tale, that's just not me. I want Bain. I want to take each breath with him by my side. The loss of Nate has scarred me, but I need to push past that pain and look at the bigger picture of my life. God gave me an amazing gift in Bain and it's up to me on how I proceed.

With tears in my eyes, I sulk into the couch. Aubrey sets her pizza down and wraps me in her arms. I lean into her and let it all out. Every twisted, pent up emotion I've been holding on to. Every ounce of pain, love, anger, hurt, regret, sadness. All of it. I let it all bleed out of my eyes. Through my sobs, I hear his name, "Bain Adams made quite an impression in Memphis earlier in the week. Now the Grizzlies are in talks with the Suns to make a big trade in order to secure the fourth pick in this year's quickly looming NBA draft. The trade is rumored to include Garrett Jones and Paul Rod, as well as the Grizzlies' thirteenth pick and a second round pick in next year's draft. Where will the ever-talented Adams end up? It's looking like Tennessee could soon be his home. I'll have live coverage of his second workout tomorrow in Tennessee. I'm Reagan Reynolds for Channel Two Sports."

Both Aubrey and I stare at the TV. Bain is moving on with his life. He's going to get drafted somewhere and move away without me, unless I make this right. Wiping the tears off of my cheeks with the back of my hand, I whisper, "Tennessee?"

"You better call him."

I shake my head and get off the couch, finally following my heart for the first time since all of this shit started.

"No." Walking into my room, I grab my backpack off the top shelf of my closet and throw some clothes inside.

Aubrey walks in and asks, "What are you doing?"

"I need to see him. Aubrey, I have to fix this. Will you drive me to the airport?"

"Arion, are you fucking crazy? You don't even have a plane ticket, or a job to pay for one for that matter."

Turning around I pull on a pair of jeans and look at her. "I can book my flight in the car on a credit card. Please drive me."

She nods her head and walks out of my room. With my backpack crammed full of God only knows what and my wallet in hand, I walk into the living room where my best friend is waiting for me with her car keys and iPad.

She glances at me briefly, then looks back down at the iPad and says, "There's a 7:15 flight. Depending on traffic, we might be able to make it."

"How do you know it's the right airport?"

"I picked the one closest to Memphis."

"Thank you, girl, you're the best." She hands me the iPad and we head out, getting into her little sports car. For a split second, I doubt doing this. It's crazy. But being brazen is what brought us together. As I select a one-way ticket, I couldn't be surer of the decision. I could call him now, but everything I need to say I have to say in person, my heart is telling me that he's there – so I follow it.

"Are you sure this is what you want to do?" Aubrey asks me.

"I know it is. Aubrey, I...I love him. I love him more than anything in this world. I'm done playing this tough card and being worried about getting my heart hurt, because you know what? All of this hurts, and being without him is unbearable. If he turns me down, the pain can't be any worse than what I'm going through now."

"Okay, girl. I love you no matter what happens and will be here for you."

"I know that, thank you. You know, Aubrey, I followed my heart with Nate and I wouldn't change a thing looking back. That's why I'm doing the same with Bain. I don't want to live life with regrets."

"I'm so happy for you. I wish I had someone like him, you're making the right choice A."

Aubrey weaves in and out of traffic, driving a bit erratically in true Jersey fashion. Glancing at the clock, I can't help but worry that I'll miss the flight. If I do, there are others. I can't go there now and start worrying before anything's happened.

With thirty-seven minutes 'til departure, the airport is now in sight.

"Please call me when you land," Aubrey says.

"I will, thank you."

"Of course, A. Good luck."

She stops in front of the departures for United and I'm thankful that the outside isn't too busy. We exchange a quick hug and I bolt. The automatic double doors open like they were made for me. Looking around, I spot the electronic kiosks, pull my phone out to get the confirmation from my email, and check in as fast as I can. This is way better than dealing with the lines of people waiting to check their bags.

Once my boarding pass prints, I have thirty-one minutes to get through security and board the plane. I take off sprinting across the terminal. I opt against a train and just run, my legs moving me as fast as I can go because there is no way I can miss this flight. I have to make it. My heart is pounding, all because I have to get to Bain. Once I finally reach the terminal, I check my ticket again and start to frantically look around for gate seven. Seven, seven, seven. *Fuck, where is it?* Then I spot it tucked in the back corner. An attendant calls over the intercom as I run with all my might. "Calling all passengers for flight 274 to Memphis. This is your final boarding call."

My legs can't seem to move me fast enough. I'm moving on pure adrenaline, then finally make it, winded. My chest is heaving and all I can think about is Bain. This is how he gets when we fuck, winded just like this.

The attendant scans my boarding pass and as I walk down the jetway, I can breathe. I made it, thank God. Upon entering the plane, I head straight for my seat. Finally I find it, tucked a few rows up from the center exit row, between two older females. "Excuse me," I politely say, squeezing in and then sliding my bag under the seat in front of me. Glancing at my text messages for the first time in God knows how long, I'm shocked. There are thirty-eight unread text messages from Bain. Scrolling to the bottom, I type out a text. *I'm ready to talk.*

My finger hovers over the keys, then hits send. Resting my head back, I close my eyes and pray he responds.

The flight attendants close the cabin doors and begin their departure procedures, walking about the plane. Then my phone chimes, *You have the worst fucking timing. I just boarded a plane back to Memphis. I'll have to turn my phone off any minute.*

My heart almost jumps out of my fucking chest — he could be on this plane. I text him back, *Me too.* When I hit send, I listen and swear I hear a phone chime that sounds just like his. Anxiety courses through me. I'm too afraid to stand up, but I begin looking around, and...I see Bain.

There he is in the front row. I can't believe I missed him when I boarded. He's so tall, leaning on the back of his seat and scouring the plane. His eyes move frantically and I'm not sure what to do. I want to run to him, but the captain turns the fasten seatbelt light on, so I text him, *I see you.* He looks at his phone, sitting back down. **Come up here right now! I have an extra seat.**

With heavy breaths I reach down and unbuckle my seatbelt. Reaching for my bag, I know there is no going back now. He knows I'm here, plus I'm flying to see him.

The plane starts to move as I get up. The moment I'm on my feet, he sees me. I watch all the wind leave his lungs. His face changes, he can't believe it just as much as I can't. But the flight attendant stops me. "Ma'am, I'm sorry. You need to get back to your seat."

"I am," I tell her, and point to Bain. She must know he has an extra seat and I practically run to him and into his arms. Our eyes never leave each other's. He tightly holds my face, pressing our lips together. Kissing him back, I wait to wake up, because this can't be real.

CHAPTER 37

-Bain-

"All right you two, you have to sit down and buckle up," the same flight attendant who tried to stop Arion from coming up here tells us. Reluctantly, I pull my lips from hers. We both sit and I lean over, buckling Arion's seatbelt, then mine. Being this close to her is unreal. She smells so unbelievable and looks even more beautiful than I remember.

Looking at her, she hasn't taken her eyes off of me for a second while I get us situated. The guy next to us is also staring, but I couldn't care less. In all honesty, I can't even fathom what is going on right now, is this for real? Looking at her, with her clear porcelain skin, she's here. She's really right here, next to me, on this plane, and the only reason that she would be flying to Memphis would be for me.

Both of us stay quiet, neither saying a word, and I wrap my hand around hers, bringing those sweet fingers to my lips. "Bain," she whispers as I set our hands back down. "I'm sorry."

I shake my head, just feeling thankful to have her in my hold. The last thing that I want her to feel is regret. "*I'm* sorry."

"Why?" she asks turning in her seat.

I lift up the armrest and grab her thigh as she rests it against mine. My dick begins to pulsate from the close contact. "Because I should've been honest with you from the beginning." I ensure that I keep my voice down, as we are on a packed plane and don't need an audience. "I knew from the moment that I laid eyes on you, I wanted you and I would take you any way I could have you." Reaching up, I run my thumb across those lovely lips, afraid my honesty is going to make her get angry with me. "So I lied to myself, just as much as I lied to you."

She inhales deeply and then lets it all out. "I think we are both a little guilty of that. Why do you think I'm here?"

I shrug my shoulders. I need to hear her say the words. I can't answer that for her, as much as I wish I could. "Bain, I've had a long time to reflect on all of this, on us and what we have, and what it boils down to is you make me happier than anyone in this world. You make me smile and love my life and make me feel again. Something I haven't known in so long. And because of all that, I fucking love you."

Taking her by the back of her hair I pull her face to mine, looking into those clear eyes. I want to make sure what she is telling me is true; in fact, I need to know in my heart. Looking deep within her, searching for something to grip on to, I know it's true when she smirks at me and says, "I love you."

"I love you too, baby. God, I love you."

The moment I speak the words, the plane takes off. The force of gravity pushes us into our seats, and she smiles at me. I can't resist telling her again, "I love you."

She kisses me as soon as I say the words. The plane gets cruising at a comfortable altitude and Arion lies against my chest. I hold her body to mine, noticing how small and fragile she is.

"How long can you stay?" I ask her, already scared that she will have to go back for work.

"Forever. I lost my job."

"What? Why?"

"Let's just say I had a really hard time without you."

"Come on, A. You loved that place."

"I know, but I couldn't make myself get out of bed and that made getting there really hard."

"I can't believe they let you go just because you were late."

"It was more than once, babe, and a few other things happened."

"I'm sorry, baby."

"Don't be," she says, pressing her lips against my chest. Her breath is warm through the fabric of my clothing.

With my girl wrapped up in my arms, I hold her tight,

as close as humanly possible without crushing her. My mind is mixed and clouded with a thousand different thoughts. Regardless of everything rushing though my mind, I pray that this is the beginning of the rest of our lives together, because in all honesty, I can't lose her again.

"You're quiet."

I look down at her before responding. "I don't know what to say and I'm scared that it'll be the wrong thing. I don't want you to ever leave again."

"I'm not going anywhere. If you'll take me back, I'm in this for forever. I never should've left. I was being scared and naïve. Bain, you're the best thing that's ever happened to me."

"Really?" I ask, looking at her, a bit surprised by her words.

"Yes. I promise no more games or hiding my feelings. I'll give you all of me."

Her words are the best I've ever heard. "All of you is all I've ever wanted. You promise no running or getting scared or anything like that?"

"I promise, and when you're ready, we seriously need to talk about Memphis."

There's my girl. "What's wrong with Memphis?"

"Do I look like a country girl?"

"Clearly you haven't explored the city."

"Please, I guarantee it's nothing compared to New York."

"True, there's nothing like New York, but don't get

too worked up about it just yet. My workout there didn't go too well. I can't be picky, baby. I have to go where they—"

She cuts me off. "We. We have to go where they tell you."

"Right. We. God, I can't believe this."

"Well, believe it, because I'm not going anywhere."

Fumbling to slide the card into the door, I can't do it fast enough. Arion is on me. Hands everywhere, hot mouth all over my skin, her tight, little cunt pressed up against me and finally the motherfucking door opens. Walking her in backwards. I drop both of our bags and kick the door closed. Looking around, the bed seems so far away.

She rips her shirt off and I grab her by the thighs dropping us to the floor. Fuck it. I need her now. Right here. I watch how relaxed she is lying there waiting for me. Leaning down, I unbutton her jeans, skimming them down as quickly as I can. The moment she's naked, her scent intoxicates me. "Fuck, you're wet. I can smell you, so sweet."

She takes her fingers, fanning them down her stomach and I watch, frozen. She wouldn't dare. Would she? Then she opens her soft pussy and begins to please herself. I've never seen her touch herself. Christ, it's hot.

"Have you touched yourself like this lately?"

She nods her head.

"Really? What did you think about?"

"You and your cock," she says, reaching over and grabbing me through my pants. I unbutton them and with urgency she get's right inside. She's barely able to get my dick out as it strains the fabric and is starting to hurt. Once I'm free, she sits up and has her lips around the head before I can even look down and see what she's doing.

She's no longer touching herself. Her hand simply rests over her sex and I lift it up, devouring the sweetness off of those fingers. Jesus, I love her. I fucking love every single thing about her. Especially how sexy she is. With her fingers in my mouth, she doesn't stop what she's doing as she bobs up and down on my dick.

Watching her move and how she makes my dick glisten, has me about to lose it. My balls tighten and before I let go, I pull away. She looks at me confused and I rip the shirt above my head. I haven't come in well over a week and I won't do that to her.

"Take your bra off," I command as I nudge the head of my cock against her waiting pussy. "Mmmmm, you're so fucking hot, Arion."

"Nothing like you," she says, running a trail of her fingers down my chest and abdomen. I pull her ass up close to me, keeping her legs spread wide, and press my cock fully inside of her. She looks up at me with the clearest expression I've ever seen. Her arms are stretched up above her, making her tits so high and perky.

With our two bodies connected like this, I know I should begin moving and fucking her. But I can't. I need to get as close as possible and this is the only way I know how, with part of me inside of her.

"What's wrong?" she asks, as I'm motionless, watching her lie in my control.

"Nothing," I respond and begin to make small pulls and pushes in and out of her.

The inside of her pussy is like nothing I've ever experienced, it's so warm and tight. I swear her body was made for mine. The way my hands feel around her hips — perfection. Or the way her skin tastes on my lips — heaven.

I'm doing my best to keep my movements slow and to take my time inside of her, but I can't. Her noises let me know that she wants more. Who am I kidding? My girl likes to be fucked. Picking up my rhythm, my orgasm won't hold back. I fight it with all of my might. My body becomes damp, and electricity pulsates through me. I do my best to watch her as I let go, she's my biggest turn on. But the force is too great. My balls erupt and with that great force, I give her part of me.

Coming inside of her sweet body that I adore so much, I faintly hear her cries of pleasure and then feel her nails dig into my forearms. Like clockwork, she lets go when I do. Our bodies knowing each other so well that they do things on their own. Looking at her sweaty skin, her chest heaves heavily. I kiss her harshly and begin moving again. I'm not done with her. In fact, I'm far from it.

nessee. It's
away the
ive for the
have any

l I reach
...ncs. "Here," I tell him,

......ung it to him.

He doesn't answer it, or look at the screen. Instead, he holds me tighter and nuzzles into my neck a little more. I smile, loving how he doesn't care who's calling him. Then it rings again and this time he looks at it. "It's James." He answers with the phone on speaker, setting it on top of the covers.

"I told you to email me." His voice is laced with annoyance.

"News like this can't wait for an email that'll take you all day to respond to. The Nets contacted me, and if I remember correctly, when you were fourteen that was the team you always dreamed of playing for."

"Yeah, and I was fourteen. What do they want with me anyways? They have Hashon."

"Not anymore. They just traded him, so I shortened your workout in Memphis to only today. You fly back tonight and have a meeting with them in the morning."

"Did you book me an extra seat?"

"Of course."

"Will you call the airline and change it to Arion's name? She's here with me. Anytime you book anything in the future, will you book her with me as well?"

"Sure thing. I was wondering why you were so civil this morning."

Bain laughs and I move, straddling his body. He engulfs me in a big, warm hug and I do the same. "Sorry I've been so negative lately. I really appreciate everything you do, James."

"Don't mention it. We'll talk more, later, and I'm sure you'll be tired of me again. Goodbye," he says and hangs up.

"Thank you," Arion says.

"For what?"

"For the flight, and telling James to book our stuff together."

"Of course. I can't spend a day without you. Will you please reconsider my offer? I want you to help James manage me."

"Come on, Bain," I whine. "Do you really want me to co-manage you, or is this about being apart and me being jobless?"

"I really want you to help manage me."

"What am I even supposed to do?"

"Just come today, watch me play, and listen to what the coaches have to say. Always keep your ears open and then we'll meet with James when we're back home to figure out how you can best help."

"I'll come today. But I can't agree on anything 'til I talk to James."

"Okay," he says kissing my cheek.

As our naked bodies lie together, his erection is hard underneath me. Christ, I've missed this. I've missed him and us so much. Moving my hips, I begin to rub myself against him. My pussy is already wet.

Reaching down, Bain stops our foreplay and guides himself inside of me. We effortlessly fit together, like two pieces of a puzzle snapping into place. Bain and I relish one another and I know that I made the right decision. What we have is more real than anything I've ever dreamed of. I've given every piece of what I am to this man. He has my heart, my future, and my trust.

Without even noticing how fast my movements are, my body begins to spiral. Then so does Bain's. He grunts violently, holding me to him by the back of my head and says, "I love you." Those words mixed with his pure passion and love, take me out of this universe.

The trembles from within finally stop and I stay placed, in my heaven, atop Bain, where his love exudes from him and into me.

"Come on, A, we need to shower and get going."

Reluctantly, I get off of him and he follows right behind me.

Finally, I take my first real look around this magnificent room. It's gorgeous. A contemporary décor in a scheme of browns and whites.

Since I'm a bit lost in the room, Bain smacks my naked ass and walks ahead of me, starting the shower.

Sitting next to Bain as we head to the workout facility, I feel nervous. What am I really supposed to say to the coaches and where do I stand? They are all going to know that I'm there because I'm his girlfriend. I don't want anyone to think he's not taking things seriously. Especially when I don't know the first thing about the game. All I know is the ball is supposed to go into the damn basket.

"Thank you for coming," he says.

"Of course, but if I'm being honest, I'm nervous."

"Don't be, babe."

"But I'm your girlfriend."

"So? You can also say you work for James. Tell them he couldn't be here on this trip so you came to make sure things go okay. If they start to ask you a bunch of questions, then you tell them firmly they might want to ask James that."

"Okay," I say as he engulfs my hand, wrapping his

tightly around mine.

"Can I ask you something on a serious note?"

"You know you can. I told you last night from now on I'm an open book."

"No matter where I get drafted, are you coming?"

"Yes," I answer right away, because I am.

"What is your gut telling you about Memphis, though?"

"Honestly, I don't know yet. Maybe we could drive around tonight and check things out?"

"Definitely. If we have time before our flight, for sure. If not and we had to decide right now. Where would you pick?" he asks me.

"I would rather stay in New Jersey to be honest. It's home to me. I've never really had a good, solid home. But right now, with Aubrey, I somewhat have that."

"I can't wait to buy you a house – a home. Somewhere you will always be comfortable."

Bain puts the car in park and I look out the window, observing the massive facility. "Holy shit, this place is fucking huge."

"Yup, now let's go see if I can concentrate with your fine ass here."

"You better be able to focus because you know I'll be at all of your games."

Returning home feels so good. I can't even put into words how much I've missed New Jersey. The weather, noises, and even the people. Who would have ever thought I would've said that? Bain is practicing with the Nets today and deep down I'm hoping that's where he gets drafted.

Checking the clock, I'm running right on time to meet with James. He agreed with Bain that there are definitely certain things I can help with, so he thought it would be a good idea for us to talk. Aubrey's working – of course she fucking is, that's all that girl does. Since coming home, I've barely had a chance to talk to her. I really want her to know how much I appreciate her support. It means the world to me.

Looking in the mirror, I've got a knee-length, black, tight dress on and a pair of heels. I want James to know that I'm taking this seriously. Before I head out, I also grab a sweater from Aubrey's closet so I look modest, and do one last scrunch on my messy, blonde hair.

James and I are meeting at a local Italian restaurant. I guess that's where you handle these types of things. On the drive, I get a call from Bain. "Hey you," I answer, so happy to hear from him.

"Hey to you. I just wanted to call and wish you good luck with James."

"Thanks, babe."

"Of course. I like hearing you call me that, A."

"Well, I'll keep trying. How's the workout going?"

"I don't want to get my hopes up, but this place is

fucking unreal."

"Really?"

"Yeah, really. I wish you could've come to this one, for sure."

"I'll talk to James about it. I mean, it is my job after all and we don't have much time before the draft. Seven days, right?"

"Yup, not long at all. Have I told you how much I love you?"

"Love you, too. I'm gonna go meet with James. Call me when you're done. Love you."

"Okay, baby, love you, too."

Walking in, I find James. He already has a table for us. Sitting in front of him is an iPad and a Blackberry box. I know already this will be a whirlwind of a meeting. With the brand new electronics, he means business. I exhale deeply, knowing all I can do is listen and pray some of this clicks.

CHAPTER 39

-Bain-

"So, we'll see you tomorrow morning?" Ron, the shooting coach asks me.

"Of course. I'm gonna rest tonight and I'll be back." I shake his hand and walk into the underground parking garage of this new facility, in the heart of downtown Brooklyn. Getting in my car, I grab my phone and quickly go to my baby's number.

"This is Ari—"

She stops and begins to laugh.

"Are you all right?" I ask her.

"Oh my God, yes. It's been a crazy day, baby. Let's just say the second I turned on the phone James gave me, it's been ringing off the hook. I guess I now answer my phone like that."

"Really?"

"Yeah, like seriously, we need to talk about a lot of things tonight."

"Can we talk on a date?"

"Of course. What did you have in mind?"

"It's a surprise. Let me run home and shower, then I'll pick you up in an hour or so?"

"Come on, just tell me where we are we going."

"Not telling you, baby. I love you, I'll see you soon." I hang up before she can get out another word. I know she's fuming and wants to know what we are doing. She's not a big fan of surprises, but tonight I want to have fun with her. I know we both need it. We went through so much, breaking up and separating and not knowing what the next day would bring. So now that we are back together and our relationship is different and stronger than ever, I want to get out and have some fun. I just want to see her smile.

Traffic is a fucking bitch trying to leave the city. I call my dad on the way, to see if everything is all set for my mom's homecoming tomorrow. He's set to pick her up in the morning and has a long trip ahead. I'm excited and proud of my mom. It's amazing that she has completed her treatment, and that it's gone so smoothly. I had so many doubts and now only hope that she stays on the right path going forward.

Thinking back on the day, I really can't believe that I worked out with the Nets. They have been my all-time favorite team and where I've always wanted to play. I can honestly say, regardless of where I get drafted, I know being fortunate enough to have visited their facility and met everyone has fulfilled one of my lifelong dreams. Not many people in the world can say they did something like that.

Fuck, most men can't even fathom being drafted into the NBA. With a smile on my face, I pull into the driveway. My dad's car is gone; he must still be working. Rushing inside, I shower quickly and dress before getting back into the car and darting to Arion's.

On the way, I stop and pick up a bouquet of flowers, just like I gave her on our first date. Walking up to her house, I knock like a gentleman, when really I want to barge in and show her I'm the boss.

My beautiful girl answers in a pair of tight ass jean shorts and a tank top.

"Hi, gorgeous," I say handing her the flowers.

She pulls me in and responds with a kiss, no words, she just holds our lips tightly together. I can't help the animalistic noises that ensue from deep within me. I'm horny as fuck and want to have my way with her right now.

"Hey, Bain," Aubrey interrupts as she walks in from her room.

Reluctantly, I pull away and say, "Hey, Aubrey, how are you?"

"Good. Are you getting excited for the draft? Your name is all over the news."

I bust out laughing. "I try and not watch that shit anymore."

"I'd do the same thing if I were you."

"It's the smartest thing to do," I tell her, then Arion

asks me, "Are you ready to get going?"

I nod my head and she grabs my hand. "Bye Aubrey," I say, then walk out into the warm June evening.

"Where are we headed?" she asks.

"I'm about to take you to my bed dressed like that."

"Not yet, you promised me a date night. You have to deliver."

"Are you saying I wouldn't deliver in my bed?"

"Absolutely not. I know you would deliver there, you always do. But I was looking forward to going out with you."

"Then out we shall go, beautiful."

We make the short drive to our special date spot and I ask her, "How did things go with James?"

"Really well. He definitely needs the help."

"Good, baby," I respond and lean over, giving her a kiss as we wait at a light. She's not looking around; she's only focusing in me. "Ready?" I ask, pulling into a parking spot. She nods her head and I hop out of the car, taking in a few deep breaths of the fresh salt-water air. Walking around, Arion meets me at the back of the car, and I can tell she's trying to get a look and feel of where we are.

The lights catch her eye as we round the corner. "Oh my God," she squeals, almost like a child would if you brought them here. I just shake my head, thankful that she's so happy. As we step onto the boardwalk, it feels nice to just be another couple in the mix of the crowd. I know after the draft, my life – our life – will never be the same.

"What do you want to do first?"

"Anything."

I chuckle at her comment, trying to decide what to do. There are shops we could go in, or we could grab a bite to eat. Looking around I see the arcade and next to it is a basketball game. Those games are nearly impossible to win for most people, but not for me. "Come on, I tell her."

Walking over, I ask the guy, "How much for one game?"

He stares at me briefly and then responds, "Five dollars for one ball or three balls for ten dollars."

Passing him a five I say, "I'll take one please."

"Are you sure?"

"I'm sure," I tell him and he hands me a ball.

Stepping back to the line, I eye the net knowing that in order to make this shot, I'll have to pop this baby up. The ball needs to drop in effortlessly and not hit one bit of the rim. I bounce it once, purely out of habit. Then eyeing my target, I shoot and make the basket look easy. It drops right through. The guy looks at me like he just got bamboozled.

Arion hugs me so excitedly and he grumbles, "Pick your prize." I know it's because no one ever wins these games, it's really just luck or skill in my case.

Arion picks a huge brown teddy bear, which I can tell she loves. It has a basketball jersey on, so I'm sure that's why.

"Thank you, baby," she says. "I had no idea you could make a shot like that."

"Never doubt my skills," I respond wrapping my arm around her waist and walking us right for the ticket counter for the Ferris wheel. Being with her like this, I think about how far the two of us have come. What used to be a mix of pain and anger has now turned to love and trust. I can see it when she looks at me, she trusts me.

Waiting in line she looks up at the massive wheel. It's lit up and one of my favorite things to do at the board-walk. But I can't keep my eyes off of her and catch guy after guy walk by staring at her. She's simply gorgeous, naturally and beautifully gorgeous, and all mine.

Resting my hands back on the hard metal railing behind me, I watch her look up at the height of the Ferris wheel. "Are you scared?" I ask.

"No. Are you?"

"Absolutely not."

We are next in line and our bucket arrives. The family that was in there gets out and Arion and I slide in. She sets her huge bear down next to her and the wheel moves a little, I can't help but want to fuck her on this thing at the top. One day I'll rent out an entire Ferris wheel and make her come from the top screaming my name.

"Do you have any idea how hot you are?" I ask, sitting across from her.

"What do you mean?"

"Look at you. For starters, your shorts are so short; I

can see your pussy when you sit like that." She closes her legs, but I tell her, "No, no, open them wider."

"Like this?" she asks, out of breath, leaning back. My cock begins to get hard and I just nod my head.

"Touch yourself."

"Bain, what if someone sees?"

"Then let them see."

She smirks at me and sticks her finger into her mouth and then inside of her shorts. "Oh, fuck, see what you do to me?" I ask as we sit across from one another. My dick is so hard that it painfully strains my jeans.

She keeps working her pussy just like I told her to. Quick little strokes.

"How does it feel?"

"Good. So good I wanna come."

The Ferris wheel must be loaded with people as it begins to make a full circle. The walls of the buckets are high and at the top is tinted glass, making me confident that no one could see her, even if they were looking.

"Then let go, baby, come for me."

Sitting back, I watch her as I rub myself through my pants. The wheel comes to a stop, we are high up and I watch her body change. Studying how her legs tremble and she clamps down tightly on her bottom lip. Relishing in the quietness of her orgasm. Goddamn, she is the sexiest thing in the whole entire world.

The wheel turns again and we head back down. There's a silent secret amongst us as it's our turn to exit.

Grabbing her hand, I take her dirty fingers and suck off the leftover sweetness that is her. That's my Arion, and the scent alone flips a switch and I have to refrain from throwing her over my shoulder. Instead, I walk quickly and with purpose back to my vehicle, where I'm going to fuck her so hard, she won't be able to look at me straight, afterwards.

CHAPTER 40

-Arion-

"Seriously, Arion, I'm too fucking big for this suit."

"Baby, come on, I know you are stressed and tense, but would you just calm the fuck down?" I snap as I try and knot Bain's black tie.

"Arion, look at me."

Looking up at him, I laugh – he's been a ball of anxiety this past week. We visited Colorado, and even when he wasn't working, he was like this. I thought the time away would calm him, but it didn't. He's so tense and how can I blame him? He's worked so hard for this day. Stepping back looking at him, just about every muscle in his body is bulging; that's why the suit feels small. "It fits perfectly and you look sexy as fuck. Would you just take some deep breaths?"

"You're so going to pay for this later if I look like my head is too big for my body on national TV."

"How's it going in there?" Bain's mom asks as she knocks on the door. Reaching back with one hand, I open it for her. She walks in with a huge grin on her face. I'm not surprised though – that's the way she's been since she came home. Bain and I have spent a lot of time over here and she's doing great. Her transition has affected both him and his dad positively.

"You look so handsome," she says with tears in her eyes.

"Oh, come on, Mom, please don't start with that." She blinks back the tears and nods her head.

"I'm just so proud of you. I've dreamt of this day for so long."

Even though she is emotional, her presence calms him. I can see his muscles relax and everything about him changes. All of his stress washes away. Then she says, "Bain, I have something for you."

"I'll give you two some privacy," I say and step away to finish my makeup.

My hair is loose and messy. Leaning forward, I apply one last coat of mascara, then spray my hair and head downstairs to grab a bottle of water.

"Hey, Arion," Bain's dad, says, sitting at the table. I didn't even notice him there.

"Oh, hey, how are you?"

"Good. How 'bout you?"

"I'm getting excited. I'm just giving Renee and Bain a moment."

"Thank you. I know I haven't said this to you before, but thank you. Thank you for everything you've done for my son. I've never seen him this happy."

"He makes me just as happy, so I should be thanking you."

Renee comes down and asks me, "Do you want something to eat before we get on the road?"

"Oh, no, I'm good, thank you though."

I notice that her eyes are red as I pass her to walk upstairs. She had to have been crying, I'm sure of it.

Walking into Bain's room, he's not in there, then I catch a glimpse of him in the bathroom. Walking up to the door, he's bracing his weight on the counter and has his head hung low. He looks at me through the reflection of the mirror with glassy eyes. "Are you okay?"

He shakes his head and hands me a silver locket on a thick chain. "She wore this when she died. I bought it for her on our eighteenth birthday."

Looking down at the locket, it's simple yet so gorgeous. It looks like something that Bain would pick out. "It's beautiful."

He nods his head and gets teary eyed. In that moment, I'm at a loss for words and just pray that I have the strength to get him through this. In my hand is a token that represents so much. It's a piece of who she was. A piece of who he was. Wrapping him tightly in my arms, we embrace. A flood of emotions works its way through me; however, I push them all away and stay strong for Bain. Today is by far the most important day of his life.

Searching for the right words to say, I finally tell him,

"She would be so proud of you."

"I know. It just fucking blows that she's not here."

"I know, baby, but you have to know how proud she is of you. I mean, think about it. You almost let this dream go, and now in just a few hours it's all going to come true."

I place the locket back in his hand. "She might not be standing with you today where you can see her, but her presence is wrapped around your soul like a cape. Embrace it and wear it with pride."

He grasps the locket tightly, holding it with all of his might and nods his head. Then gently presses his lips to it and places it in the inside pocket of his coat.

"I love you, Arion. I don't know what I would do without you."

"Well, you're never going to have to find that out. Are you ready to get drafted into the NBA?"

"As ready as I'll ever be."

I kiss him one last time before I turn on a heel to leave the bathroom. But Bain stops me, and grabs my wrist. Looking into those light, alluring eyes, I ask, "What?"

"I want another kiss, please."

Stepping to him, we tightly press our mouths together, our tongues intertwine, weaving and loving one another. Bain smells like heaven, my own personal paradise. So delicious that if this day weren't so important, I would rip his suit right off of him and devour every inch of his tattooed skin.

He places his hands firmly on my lower back, holding

my ass and pressing my sex against his cock. He's half hard and I know that we need to stop. I can see just how things would progress. I would either be against that door or on the counter and Bain would be inside of me so fast that I wouldn't know how it happened. Then neither of us would look presentable for his special day, and as much as I want him, I want today to be perfect.

"Come on, baby, let's get going."

He growls in protest, moving his lips to my neck, sucking hard.

"Bain," I snap and pull away. He smirks at me with a devilish grin.

"You started this, now you expect me to stop. You deserved that."

I look in the mirror at my neck. He sucked so hard, I swear it's going to bruise. Thankfully, there's nothing there.

"You'll pay for that later."

"I can't wait," he says and lands a firm smack to my ass. Walking into his room, I put on the ridiculous pair of heels that I bought to go with this dress. They are shiny and black and by far the most whorish pair I've ever worn.

"I fucking love those shoes."

"Well, if you behave, maybe I'll wear them for you later."

"A man can always hope."

"The car's here," Bain's dad yells from downstairs.

"Let's do this, baby."

Walking down hand in hand with Bain, his parents are both waiting for us. The smiles that radiate from them are of absolute pride. I mean, how many parents can say that their child follows a dream long enough to see it come true? For Bain, today is the culmination of all his hard work and dedication. Yeah, he might have slipped up for a couple of months, but he went through the absolute worst tragedy possible and experienced something that most people would *never* have come back from.

Walking outside, there is a huge black limo waiting and as the driver opens the door, James steps out. He's dressed to the nines and walks to us. Everyone exchanges friendly hellos and hugs. And I do have to wonder if not only Kinsey is looking down on us, but Nate too. Is he happy for me that I've found Bain?

I know that if the roles were reversed, I would want nothing more than his happiness. I pray that his soul is resting in a better place and God has him safe. Deep down, I love Nate; I always have and absolutely always will. But I truly believe that God must've needed him, so it was his time, and now Bain is my future here on earth. Holding my hand tightly, he guides me into the limo and into our future.

EPILOGUE

-*Arion*-

It's been almost two months since the draft, and Bain and I are finally getting settled into our new place in the city. I've always wanted to live in the heart of New York, but never had the means to 'til now. The New Jersey Nets drafted Bain and both of us couldn't be happier. As I sit on our brand new bed inside of our high-rise tower where we are tucked comfortably on the eighteenth floor in down town Manhattan. I work away, loving my role as his co-manager.

After Bain got signed, it's been non-stop work signing him tons of deals from underwear to clothing to nightclub appearances. There's been constant travel and now that practice is finally getting started, we are both so excited to get into the routine of NBA life. Well, as normal as it can be.

My phone rings and I grab it right away when I hear Bain's ring tone.

"Hey, babe," I answer. "How are you?"

"Good, you?" he asks.

"You know, just working my ass off. But on a good note, I haven't had to book us one flight today."

"Thank God, doesn't it feel good?"

"So good. Are you almost done with practice?" I ask him, as I walk over to the massive wall of windows that overlook the Hudson River.

"Yeah, we just showered. Do you need me to stop and get anything on the way home?"

I glance at the clock on my laptop. *Holy shit, it is after three.* "Yeah, we need food. I was gonna run to the store today and just lost track of time."

"I can go. Wanna email me a list?" he asks.

"I'll go, you had practice all day."

"I'll come grab you. I'd rather go with you anyways."

"Oh, God, this should be good. You know you always get stopped when we are out."

"It's just to the store; no one is gonna bother us," he responds.

I agree for the sake of not arguing, but I know better. We hang up the phone and quickly I change out of my sweats and into a pair of tight shorts, with a loose fitting tank top. Running my fingers through my hair, I brush my teeth, then go and look in the fridge. We really have no groceries, so I make a mental list.

Then my phone chimes with a text and I check it. *I'm downstairs, babe.*

On my way.

Grabbing my purse, I lock up the condo and head downstairs. Sure enough, the instant the elevator doors open, there is Bain. The moment we see each other, our eyes stay connected.

I can't help but want to run to him. Instead, I keep my poise and confidence 'til we are finally brought together. He shrouds his tattooed arms around me, holding me tight. But I want more than a hug, so I pull away, pressing our lips together.

"Mmmm, you smell good," he says and grabs my hand. We walk outside and there is a Lincoln town car waiting for us. The team always has them to take players to and from practice.

"Don't you wanna walk?" I ask.

"I would, but I'm tired and my knee is sore as fuck after banging it in practice."

He opens the door and we get in. There is a bouquet of flowers on the seat and I smile, picking them up and pressing my nose into them.

"How was practice? Is your knee bad?"

"It was good, and my knee will be fine. You make everything better," he says cupping my sex through my pants. "What about you?" he asks, still holding me.

"It was nice. I didn't unpack shit around the condo. But I signed you a new deal with a clothing company. The contract should be back from your attorney tonight."

"Sweet, what does this one entail?"

"A photo shoot and then you'll get a big check and a

ton of free stuff."

"Oh, God, it better be shit I like.

"It is, I promise."

"Good. Well, I was thinking today about what we should do this weekend. What do you think?"

"Stay in the condo, no electronics, and stare at the amazing views."

"I love it. I'll tell James and Benny we need some down time."

"You're awesome. You really think we could?"

"Absolutely."

"Here you are, Mr. Adams. I'm gonna pull around the block and park, just call me when you're done."

"Thanks, Carl," Bain tells the driver. "We won't be long."

We hop out and he is immediately spotted. "Bain, Bain!" two young men yell, coming over to us. We start to walk inside and they ask, "Can we just get a picture?"

Bain looks at me and I nod my head. He stops and the guys look like they are on cloud nine. One of them looks around as to find someone to snap the shot. I offer to take it for them. After a few smiles and some autographs, Bain and I finally enter the store. He grabs a cart and we move through aisle after aisle, focusing on each other. I can sense he's being recognized, but he never takes his attention off of me. I love that about him, I'm always number one in his eyes. I know I always have been and always will be.

Check out is a breeze and the drive back to the condo is quick. Once we arrive, Bain first puts his gym bag on his shoulder and then we unload the groceries. Herbert, our doorman, greets us with a friendly hello and of course starts to ask Bain how practice has been going, engaging him in talks about basketball. As I stand there with a heavy load of bags, I kiss his cheek and whisper, "I'm gonna head up, take your time."

He nods his head in agreement and I walk off. Bain really admires how nice and kind of a man Herbert is. His brother used to play in the NBA, so the two of them always get to talking about basketball. I keep my eyes on Bain 'til the elevator doors close. God I love him. Walking down the hallway on the eighteenth floor, I search my purse for the door key. Finally, I fish it out, somehow with all of the bags still in my hand.

When I slide the key into the lock, I feel a cold hand on my upper arm. I freeze and slowly turn as the voice of a ghost says, "A."

Instantly, I recognize it and am scared to turn around. As I do, I can't believe my eyes. *This is not fucking possible.* I lose all control in my arms and drop the grocery bags. The milk hits the ground and busts open, tipping and splashing all over, pooling around my feet. With my eyes locked on his, I'm shocked. Taking my hands, I press them to the sides of my face and shake my head. There is no way it's really him. "Nate?"

FOR MY READERS

I'm so blessed by each and every one of you. Thank you for reading Bain and Arion's story. I know you're mad at me and that's okay. I'm known for giving you hearts and flowers and a good ol' happily ever after. But not this time, not this story, and not these characters. It just wasn't in the cards for them – not yet. As a writer you have to follow your heart and most importantly, your characters. I did just that and hope you loved Bain and Arion's story as much as I loved writing it. You need not worry – I won't leave you hanging for too long. I'm working on *Every Heart*, a companion novel to *Every Soul*, that will be available early 2015.

In all honesty, did you enjoy *Every Soul*? I hope so, and would love to hear what you really think. Please consider leaving a review, both the Prezident and I read every single one of them and truly enjoy hearing your thoughts.

ACKNOWLEDGEMENTS

First and foremost, I need to thank my other half, William. God gave me a gift in you, in your support, and in your love. Everything you are means more to me than my next breath. Once again, this book is possible because of you. I don't even know where to start or how to say *thank you*. You've always been my number one supporter and I know you always will be. Thank you for helping me map this baby out, and for coaching me along the way. You've become the world's best beta reader and I will never share that with anyone – you're mine and damn talented. You've read this story more than I have and never protested in doing so. You never complain; you support. You never bitch; you love. You are truly a blessing. I love you to infinity and beyond, babe.

Lisa, my wonderful and amazingly talented editor, I can't even tell you how much your constant support means to me. You are one of the funniest women in the world and I absolutely fucking love working with you. When I told you we were on a time crunch, you didn't falter. Instead you calmed me down and said everything was going to be all right. Thank you for that, and for getting this baby done so quickly. I couldn't be happier with the outcome and can truly say that Bain and Arion's story is one of my favorites and I owe a lot of that to you!

Leticia, you hold a very special place in my heart and always will. I can't thank you enough for having my back and simply *supporting* me. You're always willing to help me at the drop of a hat and you're extremely talented at what you do. My books are published to perfection, because of your hard work. I'm indebted to you, always.

Corporal John Jennings, how oh how do I repay you? When I first told you my ideas, you had every possible thing to say about how that can't happen and that's not reality. *How was I supposed to know that dead bodies float?* Your attention to detail with the murder/suicide element was spot on. Thank you for making sure that I molded a perfect and believable story. I truly appreciate all of the help you gave this project.

To my sweet Pimpettes, well, if that's even the right word to call you crazy, dirty, and inappropriate ladies. Adrean, Cheryl, Christina, Lydia, Heather, Jacki, Karrie, Keri, Kim, Letty, Lindsey, Mary, Sarah, and last but certainly not least, Tevy. Thank you for all the support, smiles, and laughs. You all mean so much to me and a lot of what I do is to make each of you happy or pant! Thank you for never judging me and always loving me. Thank you for enjoying my stories and characters just as much as I do.

Lydia, girl, I hit the damn jackpot with you. You're amazing! That really is all that there is to say to sum up my feelings for you! Thank you for jumping on board with me at a moment's notice and for the constant help. I couldn't have found a better person to help introduce Bain and Arion to the world, or in a better way.

Bloggers, there are too many of you to name, but know that there are not enough words to express my gratitude. I'm indebted to you, always. The time you spend reading, reviewing, and pimping my work is unreal. Thank you from the bottom of my heart. And I could never forget my beta readers; I couldn't do any of this without you. Thank you for motivating me and digging deep into this story.

Lastly, to anyone who has ever lost a loved one far too soon and has been left searching for the answers, may you know that there is light at the end of the tunnel. Take each moment, each breath as it comes, and live in it. Ride rainbows and smile like a kid, because you never know when your time will come. Enjoy what's real. Enjoy the now. Enjoy those closest to you. XOXO, LK.